# CLAIMED BY MY BEST FRIEND'S BROTHER

CALLIE STEVENS

1

———

## CHASE

"Drive safe."

"I will."

"Take it *slow*."

"Mom, I'll be fine," I say, running my hand back through my hair. It's a classic warm late May night here in Houston. I'll need a shower when I get home to wash off the humidity.

Mom looks at me with her soft blue eyes, the same color as mine. "Chase, it's late. People drive like maniacs on the highways, so *be careful*," she reiterates, squeezing my arm.

Leaning down, I kiss her on the cheek. "I will. Love you."

She leans into my chest and hugs me. "Text me when you get home."

As we say our final goodbyes, I head to my car at the end of the driveway. My sweet ride looks out of place behind my mom's minivan. Making a mental note to get her a new car for her birthday, I get in, turn the key in the ignition, and look up at the house one last time before I pull away. Mom is still outside under the porchlight, and in the front window, Dad is flanked by my little sister and brother, Rachel and Dan, the twins. Not so little anymore at 21. But still. Little to me. They were only 4 when I was getting ready to graduate high school. Now, they're both in *college*.

Christ, I'm getting old.

I honk the horn as a goodbye and watch them all wave before pulling out into the night.

The roads are darker here at night. I'm so used to city centers across the country, across the world, that are lit up like Christmas trees everywhere you go. *Tour*. God, I love it. I already miss it. I can still hear that last cymbal crash in the back of my mind. It gets more distant every day since the tour ended, but sometimes, I remember it just right, and it sends a shiver down my spine.

Don't get me wrong, I'm grateful. I'm really fucking grateful I get to play music for a living. That's a dream. But being on the road with the band and playing my drum kit doesn't compare to the feeling of home. "Home is where the heart is" couldn't be truer than right now. Man, maybe I really am getting old.

Tonight, I'd stayed way past the time I'd planned to leave; there was just too much to talk about, too much to laugh about. Too much to enjoy. And I have the whole summer to have as much family time as possible before we record our next album.

Turning from the dark residential road into a busier intersection, I roll down the windows and pop on the radio.

"...just finished up a major world tour. I got to see it when they played here in Houston, their home city, and, let me tell you, what a show. This is Soul Sounds with 'Snake in the Grass'," the radio host announces.

I can't help but smile, hearing that opening bassline in lockstep with the kick drum and high hat. Sounds fucking good. And I don't think I'm cocky to say it. To go from garage band levels to being played on the air? We've earned it.

Even though I'm alone in my car, there is a level of embarrassment to hearing my band on the radio. My cheeks are hot by the time the song gets to the chorus, and I reach to turn the station to something else –

The next sound that hits me isn't music. It's the screeching of tires, the crunching of metal, an airbag releasing. My body is trying to free itself from my seat, being thrown around and jerked while stuck by the seat-belt, and I can't make sense of where I am in my body. Everything is dark. Pain shoots up my leg in a way I've never felt before.

Blue flashing lights and a siren. Darkness. I know I'm moving, but I'm not in control. Voices. The rumbling of tires. A glimpse of a face above me, someone wearing...an EMT uniform? Darkness. Moving, again, but this time on squeaky wheels, steadier this time. A ceiling runs by in my vision and then –

Darkness. A long, deep darkness.

The next thing I know, *really* know, I'm waking up with a dry mouth and a foggy head. I try to sit up with a groan.

A hand on my shoulder stops me. "Easy dude, woah, woah, woah."

I look up at the owner of the hand. My bandmate, Jay. "What are you doing here?"

"Everyone is here, they went for some coffee, and I only arrived a bit ago. I asked if I could see you for a second. You were in an accident, man," he says softly.

Feeling in my limbs and extremities starts to return, but my leg... "Oh, fuck, my leg, it's – "

"Your left leg," Jay interrupts.

I breathe a sigh of relief. Not my playing leg, thank God.

"You were t-boned by another driver. Fractured your leg and had to undergo emergency surgery. A couple bruises, too, but don't worry," Jay smiles goofily and points to my face. "The moneymaker's still intact."

I chuckle. "Did my folks call you?"

"Your mom called Dylan, who called Lucas, who called me. Guess I was the last to know."

"Why did she call Dylan and not you?"

"Apparently, learning your kid is in a car crash and getting to a hospital to know if he is alive messes with people's heads. Go figure. She couldn't focus so, after learning you were heading to surgery, she just went through her contacts alphabetically and he was the first to show up. Guess my parents should have called me Aaron, if I wanted to be the first, huh?"

As we are laughing, the doctor interrupts us, a bald-headed grumpy guy, and explains what's going on with my leg. He points out the fractures on my x-ray, and I wince at the image. "At least two months in a cast, off your foot," he says with finality.

"Two months? You've gotta be kidding me..."

The doctor looks at me indifferently. "I never kid."

"Charming guy..." Jay says under his breath. I would slug him in the arm if moving wasn't painful right now.

My mind is reeling, made worse by the pain meds dripping through my IV. "So, what's that mean?" I ask the doctor.

"You had a compound fracture and a comminuted fracture in the same leg. If you want it to heal quickly and correctly, you have to rest. Really rest. No strenuous activity, no exercising..."

*No drumming.* I hear it without the doctor saying it. It'd be hell to try and sit behind the kit with this cast on my leg anyway.

"I know what compound fracture is, but what is that other one?"

"It's when the bone shatters into several fragments. Here, see?" He points at a few white specks in the image. "We have to hold them together and they need to stay in their ideal position so they can heal right. So, either you rest and have your leg be good as new, or you don't, and there is a possibility we might have to go in again to fix the damage. Your choice."

Cringing at the image, I can feel my heart breaking, and so can Jay. He claps his hand on my shoulder, sighing. "Sorry, man."

I chew on my lower lip and close my eyes. This is *not* how I wanted to spend my summer off.

"I'll see if your family is outside and let them know—" the doctor says, but before he can finish the sentence, my mother bursts in, followed by Dad, Rach, and Dan.

Mom is in tears, bolting toward the bed. "Chase, oh god! Thank God you're awake. My poor baby. Look at you."

I haven't gotten a good look at myself, but from the warped reflection of my face in the IV pole, I'm a fucking wreck. "I'm fine."

"Fine? You could have been killed," she cries and wraps her arms around me. "I told you to – "

"*Be careful*, I know. I tried, but..."

Dad flanks my other side. "Thank God it's only a leg. We were terrified."

Their eyes are creased with worry. I look over at Rachel and Dan. Dan's got bedhead and is squinting in the cold, hospital light, and Rachel's wearing sweatpants, which she never does in public. It dawns on me suddenly that it's still the middle of the night, or at least, the early morning. They leaped out of bed to come here because of me.

"I mean...we thought you might be..." Dad can't bear to say the word.

I swallow. This is more serious than a summer spent on the couch. Even though my vision is hazy, I can see everyone's cheeks are tear-stained.

Jay relays what the doctor told us to my parent. They thank him profusely for being here. I owe him big time. And I need a new emergency contact. Every other 35-year-old guy has their girlfriend or wife as an emergency contact. I have *Mom*. Truth is, I had never needed it before, so I never thought to change it. The only alternative is Jay. Maybe that would be better.

"Two months. That's a lot of time, buddy," Dad says.

"You should come home. And stay with us," Mom adds.

I scoff. "Oh, come on, that just adds insult to injury. Literally."

"How are you going to take care of yourself? In that big apartment?" Jay asks.

I glare at him. *Not helping, bro.* "I'll manage."

"That's just ridiculous. You don't have to manage. We'd be happy to have you," Mom says, taking my hand in hers. Her grasp is so tight I can feel her hand shaking distantly. God, I really scared them.

Dad tries to smile to make up for their worry. "Absolutely."

"Aw, come on, Chase," Rachel finally speaks with her signature cocky grin. "It'll be fun. Right, Dan?"

Dan looks at me. Even though his eyes are tired, they sparkle. He's smiling, nodding. "We can make up for lost time."

I love them, but I don't know them as well as I could. As well as I should. They were just out of diapers by the time I headed out on my own. What would I have better to do by myself in my apartment anyway? I scan the room and smile. "Yeah. Yeah, I guess it would be fun, wouldn't it?"

The room fills with relief and excitement.

---

JAY HOLDS OUT THE CRUTCHES FOR ME, AND I carefully get out of the passenger side of his truck. He reaches for my arm nervously, and I wave him off. "I got it, I got it."

Jay pulls back his hands and holds them up, conceding. "Okay, just want to make sure you have one good leg."

I sigh and roll my eyes. When I was finally released from the hospital, Jay took me back to my apartment and helped me pack up before bringing me to the family house. I owe him big time for how great he's been through all of this.

Suddenly, a spritz of water hits me across the shoulder, and I jump back. "What the..."

Before us in the yard, Rachel's got the hose blasting, spraying it out in front of her like a madwoman toward another girl, who is bracing against the water. They're both squealing in laughter, barefoot in the yard like kids running through a sprinkler.

"Chase!" Rach cries out and drops the hose before bounding over to me. She leaps up and throws her arms around my neck.

"Woah, easy!" I say, trying not to cringe at the pain shooting up my neck from residual whiplash.

Rach drops her arms and grins ear-to-ear. "Chase, you remember my friend Jenna, right?"

I look over at the other girl on the lawn, and I can't believe my eyes. This girl – no, *woman* – this woman is unreal. Tall, even in bare feet, with dark brown waves of hair and curves in all the right places. *Holy fuck.* Her eyes clap onto mine, and I feel totally lost in a thicket of hazel.

I *don't* remember Jenna, but man, I wish I did.

She walks over to us. I feel my pulse racing. "Um...yeah, I think I do," I lie through my teeth.

"My best friend? Lives next door?" Rachel prods my memory a bit and –

"Oh yeah! Yeah, I remember Jenna," I say. "You're taller, I think." I sound like an idiot.

Jenna smiles at me. "Last time you saw me, I probably still had braces."

"And transition lens glasses," Rachel snickers.

Jenna blushes and thwaps Rachel on the arm. I can't help but let my eyes linger on her wet T-shirt. It looks like she's not wearing a bra. I grip the crutches a bit tighter.

"We were just helping out in the garden, but..." Rachel sheepishly looks at the hose that's gushing water down the front walkway.

"I'll go turn it off," Jenna says before looking at me once more. "It was nice to see you again."

I have to pause to keep from just babbling nonsense. She's so beautiful. A goddess with a honey voice and a perfect...everything. "Yeah, you too." I resist adding that I hope I'll be seeing more of her.

"I'll talk to you later, Rach," she adds, squeezing Rachel's arm. She says her final goodbyes and rushes off to turn off the spigot.

"Everyone's waiting for you inside, come on!" Rachel says and starts to pull me toward the front door.

I have to shake my head like an etch-a-sketch. Jenna's my sister's best friend, not a girl to stare at and...want. Christ, she's basically still a kid. I'll have to forget about her.

Jay follows us inside with my bag, and we are greeted by the rest of my family. There's an amazing lunch laid out on the back deck, and we spend the entire afternoon stuffing our faces and enjoying the weather. Jay and I tell tour stories while Dan talks about his football and Rachel complains about summer classes. Mom and Dad look so happy. I definitely made the right call.

The idea of Jenna is so far out of my head by the time we start cleaning up that I'm taken off-guard when I look at the house next door and catch sight of her through their dining room window. She's got her beautiful mane of hair tied up on top of her head with a pencil pressed to her lips as she pours over a textbook. I immediately feel my stomach drop, and that's when I know.

Jenna isn't just something I'm going to be able to shake off.

2

———

## JENNA

I need a cold shower. Immediately.

I don't even know where to begin. When Rachel told me her older brother was coming to stay with them to recover from a car accident, I didn't think much of it. I mean, I've met him before. Seen him now and again when he'd visit them, but I usually stayed away. Truth be told, even just seeing him from afar made me nervous. The guy is kind of famous, after all.

But up close...

No. Nope. We're not doing this. As soon as I get inside, I race up the stairs, not even bothering to say hi to my mom, who is in the kitchen, and leap into the shower. I let the freezing water drip down my body, which seems to quell my thoughts.

For a moment.

Because after the initial shock of cold wears off, I'm instantly transported to his arctic blue eyes that steeled themselves in mine. There's something about the way he looked at me that I just can't shake. *Fuck.* Chase MacAllistair is the total package. He's tall and has a full head of blonde hair with a clean beard to match. And while he's on the leaner side, he's obviously strong; his biceps bulge just by looking at them. All that drumming, I guess.

Shit! This was what the cold shower was supposed to prevent. I'm not supposed to be thinking about Chase MacAllistair like this, even if he is famous, because he's my best friend's older brother and *he's going to be living right next door*.

I shut off the shower and stand there, dripping, staring at the wall in front of me. I'm going to have to get over this feeling quickly before I see Rachel next because this just won't work.

I do my best the rest of the day to distract myself from thinking about Chase. I run some errands with my mom, do my nails, and do some reading to get ahead on next semester's coursework. But by the time dinner rolls around, I've got one thing on my mind.

Chase. MacAllistair.

I push around my fork in some mashed potatoes, and suddenly, they look like the coif of his blonde hair. I take a sip of my water, and the ice reminds me of the color of his eyes. I cut a piece of steak and think about how much I'd like to take a big bite of him.

"Jenna?"

I drop my fork, taken off guard. I find both of my parents staring at me. "W-what?"

"Did you hear me?" Dad asks with his bushy eyebrows furrowed. "I asked you a question."

I feel myself paling by the second. "No, sorry...what is it?"

"I just was wondering if you got a call back from that internship you applied for at the zoo," he reiterates, still frowning.

I sigh. "Oh. No. I haven't. I don't think I got it." I go back to pushing my food around my plate.

"You okay, chickadee?" Mom asks. "You've barely had anything to eat."

I nod, although I don't think I'm very convincing. "I'm fine."

They are both quiet for a moment. I can practically hear them exchanging a glance, it's so obvious. "Finding a job is tough. I know it's hard not to be discouraged…" Mom says in a gentle voice.

"But you'll find the one that's right for you," Dad finishes her sentence.

"Yes, exactly."

For once, I'm glad they're thinking my distance has to do with my summer job search that's proved nearly impossible. I've sent in dozens of applications to yield only a handful of interviews and no job. It's become a nearly nightly routine of them trying to keep my spirits up while I complain about how hard it feels to find work. Tonight, though, I'm not dissociating because of that.

I'm losing my mind over my best friend's much older brother.

"May I be excused?" I ask.

Mom hesitates but doesn't stop me. They've always been easy on me. Probably because I was a pretty good kid and there's just one of me, so the rules have always been flexible. Plus, I'm a grown woman…at least, legally. Sometimes, I still feel fifteen. Living at home. Unemployed for the summer.

Loser.

When I lay my head down to sleep later, I'm distracted thinking about he-who-shall-not-be-named (and no, it's not

Voldemort). Rachel never warned me that her older brother was *hot*. I guess I should have assumed, given his rockstar status, but he's a drummer! I always thought they put the sexy ones out front with the guitars. Why are they hiding him in the back?

Thank God I don't have any dreams about him. That would just make this all so much worse.

My plan for the day is to do some more job searching. I *knew* I should have taken a summer course like Rachel did. But there was just a part of me that thought I could find a job or an internship...it seems like it should be easier than this.

But first, before anything, coffee.

Like clockwork, Monday through Friday, Rachel stops by before her classes so we can share coffee on the porch. It's like we're old ladies already. It's the best. We talk about anything and everything, from the minute pop culture bullshit we see on TikTok to big-picture existential crises. Today, though, it's different.

"I need a favor," Rachel says, taking a swig of coffee.

"No, I will not go with you to the business school wine mixer," I reply teasingly.

Rachel sticks her tongue out at me. "That's not what I was going to ask about," she hisses, but then smiles slyly, "but I think you'd have a lot of fun..."

"Still no, Rach," I grunt.

She sighs. "Jenna, you need to get out more. I don't want you wasting a summer stuck inside your parents' house."

Rachel is very eager to get me a boyfriend. Ever since we started college, I've casually dated but never found someone who feels right. She says I'm too picky; I say it's just high standards. "What do you *actually* want?"

Rachel clears her throat and sits up straighter. "Well, as you know, Chase is staying with us while he recovers."

My ears perk up at the name of her brother. *What's wrong with me?*

"And so, he's just going to be resting most of the time. He's on a break from tour, so he doesn't have much to do anyway. But I'm in classes, Dan has football practice, and Mom and Dad have to go to work, so he's going to be alone most of the time," Rachel explains.

I bite my lip. I think I know where this is going, and I'm terrified.

"So, I thought, maybe...if you're not too busy...you could go and check on him? Just for a couple of minutes to make sure he's okay and not totally losing it being cooped up in the house."

My stomach drops, and I'm not sure what to say. If I say 'no', I look like a complete asshole. But if I say 'yes'...

"I don't mean to make you feel bad about not being busy or anything," Rachel quickly follows up. "It's just – "

"Yeah, of course, I can check on him." The answer spills out of me without thinking. It's a gut instinct.

A smile spreads across Rachel's face. She's got such a pretty smile. So full of life and joy. Regardless of my hesitancy, I know I've made the right choice. "I owe you big time, Jens."

"Don't mention it," I say with a slight shrug, trying to sound as casual as possible.

"Literally any time that's convenient for you, you can just let yourself in. You don't even have to stay too long. And if anything's wrong, you can just give one of us a call, alright?"

Taking a deep breath, I give her a small smile. "Alright. Sounds good."

Rachel leaps up and wraps her arms around me. "You're the best."

As I hug her limply, I hope she can't feel my heart beating wildly in my chest.

We talk only a little while longer before her ride shows up. She carpools to school with one of her friends in the business school. She gives me a wave before getting in the car, and then she's gone.

I can't believe I've just agreed to this. It was already going to be difficult to put Chase out of my mind living next door to him. Now, I've just invited more of him into my life.

*Calm down, Jenna. It's just a silly crush; you're stronger than that.*

Besides, I barely even know the guy. He could be a tyrant. After all, he's a famous rockstar. From all I know about rockstars, they're drugged out, sex-crazed lunatics. Motley Crue, Led Zeppelin...right? Not the kind of guy I'm interested in anyway.

I decide I'll check up on him around lunchtime. He's freshly out of the hospital, and I'm sure he's not in the best shape to rummage around for something to eat. It'll be half an hour of my life, *tops*. No big deal.

Before that, though, I go for a run to clear my head and help me shake off my nerves. I can't tell if I'm more nervous because Chase is *that* attractive or because he's Rachel's brother. He's completely off-limits. Plus, he's a grown man with a whole career. I'm just a kid. It's so ridiculous, I have to laugh about it.

Maybe Rachel's right. I need to get out more.

3

———

CHASE

I WAKE UP TO THE SOUND OF KEYS JANGLING AND cabinets opening and closing in the kitchen. I reach for my phone and try to look at the time, but the numbers blend together on the screen. These pain meds are really messing with my head. When the world stops swirling around like paint on a canvas, the time comes into focus.

Barely past half past noon.

I frown. No one should be home right now.

I sit up from my place on the couch where I've been napping on and off all morning, grunting as I go. This accident has not helped with the feeling of getting old now that I'm basically incapacitated. I look through the doorway from the living room into the kitchen but can't see who's inside. I reach for my crutches and heave myself off the couch. It takes a couple of attempts at first. I'm still weak and even though there's no one watching, it's an embarrassing state to be in.

I go to the doorway of the kitchen; immediately, my jaw drops. It's Jenna. In the flesh. In the house with me. Alone. And she's just as beautiful from behind as she is in front.

Her jeans show off her round, buxom ass and her hair falls in rivulets down her back.

"Um. Hi," I say.

Jenna jumps and almost loses her grip on the plate in her hand. "Oh my god!"

"Sorry! Sorry, I didn't mean to scare you," I apologize.

She holds the plate to her chest, taking a deep breath. Then, she draws her gaze to me and she smiles. "I didn't know you were awake."

"Yeah, I just...just got up," I say. I run my hand through my hair, trying to inconspicuously rearrange my bedhead. "W-what are you doing here?"

Jenna gestures to the counter where there's a casserole dish set out. "Rachel wanted me to stop by and check on you. Have you eaten lunch yet?"

I lick my lower lip. The meds have made me less hungry, but I could definitely eat. "No, I haven't."

She smiles. "Oh good. Well, my mom made a meatball casserole for you and – "

"You don't have to...that's really generous," I say. I know I'm flushing. This is so embarrassing. "But I'm fine just making myself a sandwich or – "

"No, you should rest," Jenna cuts me off and waves her hand. "You take a seat."

"You really don't have to do this," I continue, stepping closer to her, but not wanting to get so close that she feels uncomfortable.

Jenna looks at me like I'm crazy. "I'm literally just going to heat it in the microwave. It's not Gordon Ramsay over here."

I can't help but laugh. "Alright, alright. As long as it's not taking up too much of your time."

"It's not," she says, snatching a serving spoon out of the

utensil holder by the stove and jerking it toward the kitchen table. "Now, sit. You need to be off of that leg."

I can tell Jenna takes no shit and that makes me smile. A girl her age needs that type of energy to make sure she's not getting fucked around with. I bet she and Rachel give all the boys hell. I follow her instructions and, sure enough, just a minute of microwaving later, Jenna puts the plate out in front of me. A casserole isn't something that necessarily looks appealing, but it smells delicious and tastes just as good. "Wow. This is great."

"My mom will be happy to hear you liked it," she says, popping the casserole dish into the fridge.

It feels weird for me to be sitting here eating while she's up on her feet. It's nice to be taken care of, but I don't want her to feel like she's serving me. "You want to sit?"

Jenna hesitates long enough that I immediately try to retract my offer. "Only if you aren't busy. I know you've probably got a lot going on, I just thought – "

"I could sit for a bit," she says with a bright tone in her voice. She sits across from me at the table, and I'm only slightly regretting asking her to sit because now it feels like we're on a mediocre date in my parents' kitchen. Complete with awkward silences and all. "How are you feeling?" Jenna asks.

I raise my eyebrows and grunt. "I've been better. I honestly don't mind the pain as much as the meds. They make me feel so cloudy."

"Things could be worse, I guess," she replies, the corners of her lips perking up in consolation.

"Oh, totally," I manage between bites of food. Turns out, I'm starving, but if I eat too fast, I know I'll start getting nauseous. "I'm not complaining, though. I'm glad I came out with my life. My car was totaled. So, I guess..."

"You can complain," Jenna says. "It sucks, you have every right to complain."

I pause and look at her. She's smiling at me, sympathetically, and while I usually feel like people are pitying me when they smile at me like that, I can tell she's not. It's something behind her eyes. Like she's not sorry for me, just sad about the circumstances. I realize I've been staring at her too long and look back at my plate. Dropping my fork, I lean back in my chair, looking out the sliding glass doors that lead out the kitchen onto the back deck. It's a beautiful day outside. And it makes me sick to think I can't enjoy it the way I was planning on it. Hikes, bike rides, seeing concerts, going out with friends, *drumming*...all taken away from me in barely the blink of an eye. "I'm disappointed," I blurt. "I'm grateful, but I'm disappointed."

"That makes a lot of sense," Jenna replies.

*Fuck*. I've been bearing my soul to this girl I barely know, my sister's best friend who is really just a kid, except for some reason, every time I look at her, my mouth feels dry and I lose the ability to make coherent sentences. "I just didn't expect it. I know it sounds stupid."

"No, not at all. That's what makes life so unpredictable and complicated. We always want unexpected things to happen, but when they do, the timing is always bad and it's not the kind of unexpected thing you want. Like a car accident or a root canal instead of – I don't know – winning the lottery or falling in love or something," Jenna replies. She explains a lot with her hands as if she were painting a picture in the air.

I chuckle. "Right. Exactly. I also recently had to get a root canal, how did you know?"

Jenna giggles, her eyes squinting together. I cannot look

at her. She gets cuter by the minute. "Man, you've had a rough go of it."

"Tell me about it," I reply dryly.

"Well, I know your family is happy to have you home. Rachel couldn't stop talking about it," she says.

"Yeah, that's definitely a plus."

"What do you think you'll do with all your time?" she asks with a slight lift of her eyebrow.

I can't help making a sour face. "Um...well. Probably a lot of catching up on shows I've missed over the past couple of years. Maybe...um..."

"Oof, sounds like we need to get you a hobby," Jenna teases. "You can't binge-watch for two months straight."

I drum my fingers on the table as I think of things I could possibly fill my time with. "Fair. You have any recommendations?"

"Hmmm...your hands might be too big for knitting or crocheting..."

"Do I look like the knitting or crocheting type?" I ask with a roll of my eyes.

Her jaw drops, smiling. "Listen, I don't judge! Anyone can be into fiber arts."

"*Fiber arts?* Is that what it's called?"

Jenna scoffs at me and looks away. "Finish your casserole. I'll think of something."

"Yes, ma'am," I answer and focus on eating as much as I can before the nausea hits. For such a sweet-looking girl, Jenna's got a little bite to her, and I like that. She can stand her ground. Women twice her age can't do that sometimes. I'm grateful Rachel's got such a strong-willed friend to balance out her enthusiasm. My last bite of food feels thick going down my throat now that Rachel's on my mind again because it reminds me I need to keep myself in check. Jenna might be beautiful and she might be fun to talk with, but that's as far as it goes. I push the plate away from me and sigh.

Jenna looks at me, surprised. "You're done already?"

"Meds," I say sheepishly. "Promise, it's good."

She takes the plate and goes to the sink to clean it. "I was going to say, for a guy your size, I expected you to have at least two helpings."

I swallow at the thought that Jenna's evaluating me just as I'm evaluating her. Although, that's natural for anyone meeting a stranger. Right?

"You want to go sit on the deck? It's such a beautiful day and I'd hate for you to miss it," Jenna announces once everything's been cleaned up.

I look out at the back deck again. "Yeah, sure. I'd love that. I might need a little help but..."

"That's what I'm here for," she says cheerfully.

I grab the crutches and Jenna opens the door for me, but I insist she go through first. "I can manage the door," I promise, although it does prove harder to slide it closed than I imagined. I play it cool, hoping she didn't notice.

"Where would be most comfortable for you?" she asks.

"Probably the lounge so I can put my leg up," I say, chewing on my lower lip. I prop up the crutches on a nearby table and grab onto the back of the lounge. I try to twist my body so that I can just plop into the chair, but it's much further down than I anticipated.

"Woah, woah, woah, let me help," Jenna tries to stop me.

"I've got it, really," I say, although I'm pretty sure I don't totally "got it".

Suddenly, I feel her hand slide across my back to my underarm, sending an electric current down my back. She places her other hand on my ribcage and pulls my weight into her.

"Listen, I'm heavy, don't hurt yourself."

"Look who's talking," she spars back. "Come on, I can take it."

I hesitantly put my arm around her neck and lean into her. Despite telling myself I have to resist Jenna, having her this close to me brings back all the feelings seeing her yesterday in the yard brought out in me. And then some. I can smell her now, her fruity shampoo and a spritz of some sort of perfume. It's intoxicating. I let her lower me down into the chair carefully as I prop my leg up on the lounge and I'm struck by how strong she is. How safe her arms feel.

"There you go..." she coos before releasing me. As soon as her touch is gone, my heart sinks.

I've got to get a grip.

Jenna suggests we put on some music. She puts on some sort of gentle acoustic music and sits on the opposite lounge.

"You don't have to stick around, I know you've got stuff to do," I say, trying to get her to leave so I don't end up thirsting more for her.

She shrugs. "I don't mind." Then, she looks at her hands. "Honestly, I don't have as much going on as I'd like."

"You're not taking summer classes like Rach?" I ask.

Jenna shakes her head. "No, I'm actually ahead on my coursework. And my major doesn't offer much in terms of summer classes, so..."

"What are you studying?"

She purses her lips like she's ashamed to say it. "Wildlife conservation."

I gasp. "What? That's so cool."

"Yeah..." she says half-heartedly.

"Or not. Sounds like you hate it," I say with a frown.

Jenna flushes, and I notice she has a patch of freckles on her nose bridge. "It's not – I *love* it. I really do, it's just…I was hoping to get a job or an internship this summer. And it's such a competitive field it's nearly impossible to find something. All the jobs are going to people with their master's degrees and PhDs…I don't even have my bachelor's yet."

I can tell she's frustrated. I won't linger on it. "How'd you choose that? You must be really into animals." Add that to the list of stupidest things I've ever said.

She nods. "You know how everyone kind of goes through an animal phase?"

"Like horse girls," I grin, resting a hand on my stomach.

"Okay, let me be clear, I've never been a horse girl," Jenna says, holding up a finger to shush the thought. "I was a bird girl. I still am."

I can't hold in my laugh. It's big and hurts my ribs. "A *bird* girl?"

"Yeah! I like birds. Specifically, birds of prey. You know, a lot of them are really endangered," she says. "Vultures, hawks, eagles…so, I used to read a lot about them, and they're really important to our ecosystems, just like any other animal. But birds always get left out. So, I like birds."

I can't say I expected a girl like Jenna to be "a bird girl" as she calls it. Although, I should get better at not judging books by their covers. I can sense her passion when she talks about it and while I can't say I know a lot about birds, I think Jenna would be a really good teacher. "Are you a bird-watcher, then?"

Her face brightens. "Oh yeah." Then, she points out at one of the trees. "You see up there? That big nest? It's a Cooper's Hawk nest. I've been waiting for her eggs to hatch."

I squint, spying the brambly thicket high up in the tree. "Wow. That's really fucking cool, Jenna."

Jenna blushes again. "Yeah. Well. Anyway. It's hard to find jobs in the field right now. So I'm kind of just... around this summer."

"Sounds like you need a hobby too," I muse.

She smiles at me. "Yeah, I guess you're right."

We both go quiet, the music taking up the space in our silence. I feel my head swimming from the meds again, and my eyelids are growing heavy. *Fuck.* I don't want to fall asleep, but sometimes, it's impossible.

"Thanks for coming by," I say quietly.

"Don't mention it," she says sweetly.

The day is a perfectly warm blanket and the natural soundtrack of birds chirping and the occasional plane passing overhead is like a lullaby. "You know..." I know I shouldn't ask. I know I shouldn't even put the idea into the universe. But I can't help it. "You're always welcome to stop by. It's nice to have company. Maybe we can come up with a couple of hobbies to pass the time."

Jenna doesn't reply right away, and I get a feeling that maybe she is about to turn me down. But then, she says, "Sure, I definitely will."

I try to hide the smile on my face. "Cool."

"Cool."

Even though I want to, I'm unable to stay awake very long.

The next thing I know, there's a hand on my shoulder.

"Bro. Bro, wake up."

I slowly lift my eyelids and find myself face to face with Dan. He's still in his football uniform and his cropped blonde hair is so sweaty it looks like he's just taken a shower. "Hey man...what time is it?"

"Dinner time," he says with a lopsided smile. "How long have you been out here?"

I sit up as quickly as I can, but this doesn't suit my leg. A pain zips up my side and I gasp.

"Easy, man. There's no fire, relax."

I look around frantically, a hand against the lock of my cast. The sun has moved in the sky and now the world is bathed in golden twilight. From inside, comes the clanking of dishes and the voices of my parents and Rachel.

"Fuck, I don't know. Hours, I guess."

"Jeez, those meds are intense," Dan says, shaking his head. "I'll help you up."

I wave him off. "Thanks, man, but I'm good, I'll be in in a minute."

"Suit yourself," he says with a shrug and then disappears back inside.

I sigh and look over at the lounge chair that now sits empty beside me, where Jenna was just hours before. And a feeling I know I shouldn't have overcomes me.

I'm so excited to see her again.

## 4

## JENNA

"Knit one...pearl two..." Chase repeats to himself under his breath, fumbling with the shiny pink knitting needles my mom loaned me. We're starting off easy with a scarf, but even that's proving to be difficult. "I think you're right, my hands are too big. Or my fingers..."

I swallow, watching his hands attempt to tame the yarn. Chase has huge hands and his fingers are long and thick. I bet they're great for playing the drums, but knitting *is* proving as challenging as I suspected.

"You're doing so much better than me," he says, nodding toward my attempt at a scarf.

I drop my knitting on the coffee table in front of me. "I guess knitting is out, then, huh?"

Chase grins through his beard. It's gotten a bit scruffier over the past week. "Now, hold on. Give me a chance to get it right."

"Okay, as long as you're having fun."

Chase zeroes in on the needles again, his tongue touching his teeth as he focuses. "*Fun* isn't the right word. I have a vendetta against this yarn now."

I laugh and get up. "I'm going to make some coffee. Want some?"

"Yeah, thanks," he says without looking up from his work.

I go into the MacAllistair kitchen and start to brew a pot of coffee. It's a good moment to pause and reflect on how the hell I got so comfortable here.

Sure, I've been spending time in this house ever since... well, forever. Rachel and I have been friends since we were in diapers. Since we were *fetuses*. It's only natural that the MacAllistair house is home away from home for me. I know where everything is, I have my own set of keys. Chase, however, is new to the scenery.

It's only been five days, but since I brought Chase lunch on Monday, I've returned every day around the same time. Each day, I've stayed just a little while longer than the last. This has mostly been determined by Chase's ability to stay awake since his meds are running him ragged. Otherwise, I'd probably never leave.

But I can confidently say that we're just friends. And that's the way it will be. The way it will *have* to be. I'm friends with both Rachel and Dan, it's only natural I'm friends with Chase too. I'm surprised by how much I have in common with a man in his mid-thirties. We seem to be able to talk about almost anything. And even on the things we don't connect on, we're both curious. I let him talk about drums and his band and he asks me questions about school and birds. Ever since I told him about the hawk, he's asked me to update him. I even brought my binoculars over yesterday.

Today, though, it's raining, which means we can't be out on the deck like we usually are after lunch. We've been sequestered to the living room so Chase can prop his leg up on the ottoman.

My haze is broken by a clacking sound from the other room. I peek through the kitchen door into the living room and find Chase has taken his needles out of his sloppy attempt at a scarf and is drumming them on the coffee table. A laugh escapes me. He stops immediately, looking over his shoulder at me. "What?" he asks with a lopsided smile.

Okay. We're just friends. But if that's going to stick, he can't smile at me like that because it makes my insides melt. "You really are a drummer," I reply.

Chase looks at the knitting needles, flushing a bit. "Is it obvious?"

"You don't have to stop on my account," I say apologetically and go back to pour us two mugs of coffee.

"No, it's alright," he says from the other room. "It's not the same anyway." There's an edge of sadness in his voice.

I watch the steaming brown liquid pool into a pink mug that's got the phrase 'Best Mom Ever' written on it in gold script. Underneath all the friendly conversation and wooziness from the meds, I can tell there's something deeper going on. The loss of his freedom, not just literally, but mentally and creatively too. He can't follow his impulses like he's used to. That must be hard.

He needs distractions.

"Hey, want to put on a movie?" I ask, walking in with the two mugs of coffee.

Chase shrugs. "Sure, although I warn you, I might fall asleep."

"Ah, the joys of getting old."

He scoffs, "Hey!"

"Here, this'll help." I hand him the cup of coffee, and in the exchange, his fingers brush up against mine. They're rough with calluses from drumming. My breath catches inside me, but I shake it off and return to my seat at the opposite end of the couch.

Chase thanks me and takes a sip. Relief passes over his face, the buzz of caffeine already hitting behind his eyes. "Okay, what do you want to watch?"

"I don't care," I shrug. "You pick. You're the one in pain," I add with a melodramatic wail.

"Just you wait, I'm going to find something to tease you ruthlessly about, bird girl," Chase shoots back and reaches for the remote on the coffee table. It's just far enough out of reach that he has to strain, his tongue sticking out over his teeth.

I quickly maneuver my foot and push it out of his grasp. He laughs. "Oh, that's how we're going to play..." His voice is low, almost a growl if he wasn't being playful. If my insides weren't already melted, now they're soup.

"Nope," I cut off the game before it starts and toss him the remote. "I'm just an ass. Here."

Chase takes the hint. No games. He turns on the flat screen on the opposite wall and starts scrolling through the streaming options. I had expected him to gravitate toward something...harder? If not an action movie, maybe a crime drama? Or even a documentary? But no, Chase is looking at...

"Romcoms?" I blurt.

He stops scrolling and looks at me bashfully. "You don't like romcoms?"

"I mean...yeah. I do. Rachel and I watch them a lot."

We're both quiet and he continues scrolling.

"Do *you* like romcoms?" I ask with a frown.

"No, I just thought that's what you'd like," Chase replies, but I can tell that's not the whole story. "Plus...

they're comforting. They always have a happy ending, right?"

I smile. So, the gruff rockstar likes a happily ever after. That's so adorable.

*Stop it, Jenna.*

Chase eventually settles on two options. "Okay, well, *When Harry Met Sally* is a classic. But *How To Lose a Guy in Ten Days* is – "

"Also, a classic."

He looks at me like I have two heads. "No, it's not."

"Yes, it is. It came out nearly twenty years ago!"

Chase goes pale. "Oh my god. You're right. It's..." He gulps audibly. "Vintage."

"Just like you," I chirp. I'm met with a throw pillow to the face, which I thoroughly deserved.

We descend into laughter and a bit more light-hearted arguing before Chase makes an executive decision and puts on *When Harry Met Sally* after I admit I've never seen it. "Oh, you must. You *absolutely have to* see *When Harry Met Sally*. For Meg Ryan alone."

"Is Meg Ryan your type?" I have to admit, I'm curious. From what I understand, musicians can have any girl they please. I have to wonder if he has a preference or if it's just whoever's most eager.

Chase doesn't reply right away. He screws his lips together, clearly thinking hard about it as the movie begins.

"You're telling me you wouldn't sleep with Meg Ryan?" I ask incredulously.

"Woah, woah, woah, Jenna," Chase says. "My 'type' is different from who I'd sleep with."

I frown. "How so?"

Chase turns his gaze toward me. His perfect pools of ice blue send goosebumps all down my arms. "Your type is like your holy grail. Right? The *type* of person you want or gravitate toward. Who you sleep with sometimes surprises you."

I snort and look away to make sure he doesn't see the blush rising to my cheeks. "I don't think I want to know the people you've slept with who've surprised you."

"Oh, come on, don't you have that person you look back on like, 'Huh...don't know how that happened,'?"

I bite the inside of my cheek. I don't. Because I've never slept with anyone in my entire life, let alone someone I could reflect on as if they're a good story to tell at parties.

As if sensing my discomfort, Chase drops the subject. The coffee doesn't seem to help Chase because he's out like a light not long after the movie starts, letting out heavy breaths of sleep. I continue watching the movie, and right off the bat, I'm hit in the face by one of the first scenes, when Billy Crystal turns to Meg Ryan and says, "Men and women can't be friends because the sex part always gets in the way."

I look over at Chase for the briefest moment and then shake it off. Maybe when there isn't so much baggage, that's true. But Chase and I are too similar and too different simultaneously. We share too much, like the twins and the neighborhood, and we don't share enough, like our different generations and our lifestyles. For Harry and Sally, it makes sense that they would inevitably come together.

For us...well, that'd just be ridiculous.

5

---

# CHASE

"So, how's the leg? Give me an update," Dylan's voice comes through the phone crisp and clear.

I sigh. "Um, it's good. I saw my doctor a few days ago. Says it's healing properly and I should be on track to get the cast off sooner than later, so..."

"That's great, man. I'm glad to hear it," the guitarist says. The smile is apparent in his voice.

"How's everything with you? Now that you're a taken man and – "

"Oh, it's *great*," he replies without even letting me get the question out. I don't blame him. Things have been on the up and up for him for a while. "But we don't need to get into all that, I want to hear about you."

I close my eyes. I've been nursing a headache all morning. "No, really. I need the distraction."

Dylan hesitates and then launches into all the romantic and gushy minutiae of his life. It takes my mind off having felt like I've been stuck on this couch for the past two and a half weeks and that life is just passing me by. The only times I've left the house are for follow-up appointments or to go sit on the deck. It's pathetic.

The only thing that's been keeping me sane are the visits from Jenna. I've gotten used to her, after that first week when hearing her keys in the door made my heart beat like the marching snare drum at a hundred and twenty beats per minute on steroids.

Don't get me wrong, being around my family is great too. But family comes with all the baggage of being a family. There's always an undercurrent of drama about. Like the other night when Dan's football pants turned pink after Rachel accidentally put a bright red towel in the washing machine with them. The house practically turned upside down with everyone at each other's throats. Or when Dad used up the last of the eggs and put the empty carton back in the fridge by accident, leaving us eggless the next morning.

These things always get smoothed over and, for the most part, things are nice. We talk for hours on end, watch movies, play games. But most of the day, I'm on my own, and on top of that, I can't help feeling like an outsider. After all, Rachel and Dan still live at home. It's been *years* since I've lived with them. So, even though I'm a member of the family, I'm also a guest. I feel like I'm tiptoeing around (as best as I can with the use of only one of my legs) trying not to be too much of a nuisance.

Jenna seems to feel more at home here than I do. And that's...it makes things more complicated. Sure, we're friendly. I'd call her a friend by now. But I can't help but see her the way I did the day we were reacquainted on the front lawn. Seeing her move around the house like she's a member of the family just reminds me how off-limits she is.

Not that I'd ever try anything.

"Chase? Chase, did I lose you?" Dylan's voice pops back into my ear. I realize I haven't been listening.

"Hey, man, sorry, I just…I zoned out for a bit there. Tell me again…what you were saying."

Dylan chuckles. "Don't worry about it. Me and the boys will have to make time to stop by and see you. Then we can do all this catching up. You still need your rest."

I close my eyes and let my head fall back. I feel like such an asshole. "I'm sorry, D."

"No reason to be sorry. You just focus on getting better."

"Trying."

We say our goodbyes and hang up. My hand tenses around the phone and my jaw goes tight. I *hate* this. I hate that this fucking happened. And I'm stuck here with my leg in a cast. Can't drive, can't exercise, can't play the drums like I want to, *like I need to*. I'm tired of being grateful I came out of the accident with my life because it still feels like so much of it was taken away.

My phone buzzes in my hand and reflexively, I throw it at one of the armchairs. I'm tired of being reminded of the life outside and I'm tired of being checked up on and coddled and my head hurts like hell.

And then, I hear the jangling of keys outside the front door. Jenna.

I've never dreaded seeing Jenna, but I don't want her seeing me like this. I'm unshowered and I'm angry. It's just not a good day.

I shoot up off the couch, grabbing my crutches and rushing to the door. I've become a master of these things. They truly feel like extra limbs at this point. I open the door before Jenna can; I'm met with her on the other side of the door with her eyes open, wide and confused. Her hair is tied up in a patented messy bun, the one I've seen her tie together when she's thinking hard. And she's wearing a tight tank top that she has tied at the waist and shorts. She looks... well, she always looks amazing.

"Hey," Jenna says, with an unsure smile. She's got her binoculars in one hand. "I saw some activity at the nest, I think it might be – "

"Listen, today's..." I start, but then close my eyes. The sunlight is making my headache worse. I must look like a hermit who's just come out of his cave. "Today's not a good day."

She looks up at me and frowns, her forehead crinkling a bit at the center. "Oh."

"I'm sorry you came over and I – "

"Are you okay?" Jenna asks before I can explain.

I want to say "no" but then she'll probably ask me what's wrong and I don't have the stomach to tell her. "Yeah, I'm fine, just. Bad headache today. Won't be much fun."

Her lips curl into a smile. Her lips are plump and pink. I can't help but stare at them. "Well, you at least have to eat. How about I fix you something and then – "

"I'm not helpless, I can do it myself," I say. It comes out harsher than I mean for it to. And the way her face crinkles under the weight of my words crushes me. "I'm sorry, I – "

Jenna's hazel eyes dart away from mine. "It's okay, I know it must be hard."

"I'd just..." My mouth is dry even saying this. "I'd rather be alone today, Jenna."

"Okay," Jenna replies, calmly. I can tell I've hurt her. *Goddammit.* She takes a step back. She looks so young with disappointment on her face, and I remember she's still pretty much just a kid. I was basically just a kid too at twenty-one, doing stupid shit, playing in a band, surviving off ramen and cheap beer.

I force a smile even though I know it must look pained and hollow. I expect her to turn around and go, but in the gentlest manner possible, she pushes past me into the house and goes into the kitchen. I'm too confused to react at first, just left standing there, staring out the open door onto the front steps as if I've been ding-dong-ditched.

"Close the door! You'll let the mosquitoes in!" Jenna calls from the kitchen. I can already hear her rustling around, gathering whatever's necessary for today's lunch.

I close the door and hurriedly crutch my way to the kitchen. I can't help it. I'm angry. "What the hell are you doing?"

Jenna doesn't turn from her work. It looks like she's putting together the leftovers from the spaghetti dinner Mom made last night. "I'm putting together your lunch. What does it look like?"

"I told you I – "

"And I ignored you."

I feel a ball of fire erupt in my gut. Who does this little girl think she is? I don't know what I ever saw in her; she's just as stubborn as Rachel. She's just another kid sister to have to deal with. "Excuse me?"

She puts the dish in the microwave and sets it to reheat. The machine drones to life. Jenna turns back to me. "I ignored you," she repeats.

"I said I can take care of myself."

Jenna crosses her arms. "I know."

"So, what don't you understand about that?" I reply. I know I'm being mean. I don't know if I care anymore.

"I understand it plenty. But just because you can doesn't mean you have to."

And for some reason, *that* sets me off. "No, no. I *do* have to. I'm a grown fucking man Jenna. Just because I have –" I hold the crutches and shake them for emphasis, "—these fucking things doesn't mean I'm a helpless child."

"I know you're not helpless," she repeats, furrowing her brow and breaking her cool exterior.

"Then why are you barging in here making me lunch?"

"I didn't *barge* in here – "

"Um, yeah, you *literally* did."

The microwave goes off, loud and angry. Jenna grabs the plate and sets it on the table. "Why don't you eat something?"

"Oh my god."

"I don't know why you're getting angry with me."

The fire in my gut has consumed almost every part of me. I can feel it shaking behind my eyes. "Because you're not fucking listening and you're treating me like a child."

"I'm *not!* I'm just trying to help!" she shouts back.

"You can help me by leaving me alone! I asked you to leave, so leave!" I yell. It's louder than I anticipated.

Jenna's shoulders tighten; I notice her eyes are swimming now. "I didn't realize my being here was making you so upset."

The fire in me dies out immediately. All I want to do is go to her and hold her and apologize. But that's not...that's not what we have. Not who we are. "That's not what I meant at all...not at all..." I lean against the counter and drop my head. "Fuck." I run a hand over my face, feel how long my beard has gotten. "No, you, Jenna, you don't make me upset at all. Like, you make me feel the exact opposite." Shit, I'm saying too much. "I mean, having you here and getting to hang out with you takes my mind off everything going on in my head."

I look back at Jenna and she's smiling now, a small smile, but still, it's better than her being on the verge of tears.

"I'm embarrassed," I say plainly.

She lets out a snort of laughter as if I've said something objectively funny. "What for?"

"All of it. This is embarrassing. To need so much help all the time. I think it's getting to me."

Jenna shakes her head. "That's ridiculous, Chase."

"No, it's not," I say coldly.

"What I mean is..." she says, recalibrating. "We're supposed to help each other. And sometimes, we need a lot of extra help. And other times, we're the ones giving a lot of extra help. You know what I'm saying?"

I sigh. She has a point. I've been the rock for the guys at various points in their lives. For Rachel after her first breakup. For Dan when he didn't make the football team his first year of high school. "Yeah, but – "

"Nope, no buts!" she interrupts. "You deserve it just as much as anyone else."

I can't help but smile. Jenna's so adamant about it that it's hard not to agree with her. "It's just a lot of help, don't you think? I mean, I'm in everyone's way. And Rachel's made it a chore for you to come by every day and – "

"You're not a chore, Chase. I love coming to see you," Jenna says with such genuineness that I have to keep myself from smiling.

I purse my lips and look away. "If I could just drum, I think that would help. You know? At least I could practice or create something the way I really know how. And it would take my mind off things."

"Who said you can't?" Jenna replies.

I chuckle and point to my bum leg. "Um, this guy. Plus,

my old drum kit is in the basement, would be a pain to get downstairs."

Jenna scans the kitchen quickly. "Hold on." She goes to one of the cupboards below the counter and pulls out a big stockpot.

"What are you doing?"

"We're going to – "A saucepan clatters onto the counter. "—get you drumming."

I realize what she's doing. "Oh my god. You're not doing what I think you're doing, are you?"

"What do you think I'm doing?" She looks up at me with a glimmering, secretive smile.

God, she's such a delight. "I haven't played drums on pots and pans since I was in diapers, Jenna."

"It's better than not playing at all, isn't it?" she asks. In half a minute, she's emptied out the cabinets of all the pots and pans. Jenna stands to her full height again and tosses her dark hair over her shoulders, undoubtedly pleased with herself. "Come on, MacAllistair. I want to see your drumming skills in action."

The way my last name comes out of her mouth scares me. I feel my cock jump in my sweatpants and hope she doesn't notice. *Down, boy.* I try to think about my grandmother's dentures to distract myself.

"Come on, what are you waiting for?" she says, holding out a big wooden spoon to me.

"Now, hold on," I reply and pick up the big stockpot. "If we're going to do this, it's got to *look* like a drum kit."

Jenna gestures as if to give me the floor. "Show us how it's done."

I test the pots for their sound and do my best to set them up accordingly. The snare, the toms, the high-hat, and cymbals. "Bass drum I use my foot for, so that's going to be your job," I say to Jenna, giving her a plastic ladle for the deep, wide pot that's best suited to emulate a bass drum.

Her face screws together. "I don't know the first thing about – "

"I'll teach you. We'll start slow. On a four count. Come on."

On the kitchen island, with the makeshift kit, I start a simple drumbeat. It's easy enough for me that I can nod to Jenna each time she needs to bang her drum. She's getting it and it's so cute to see her so focused, wanting to make sure she's getting it right. When she messes up, she huffs and becomes even more determined.

"Something more complicated..." I start adding a few improvisations to the beat.

Jenna follows along great. I encourage her to loosen up and she starts playing along with the bass line.

"Now we're getting somewhere..."

It's not a drumkit, but it'll do, and the sounds have become their own sort of music. I can imagine the boys fleshing a song out around it. They'd probably laugh at me if I said I wanted to bring pots into the studio.

I start to pick up the pace and Jenna tries to follow along, but now that I'm in the groove, I'm not worried about her following along. Faster and faster until she's completely flustered and unsure when to hit her pot and starts laughing. "I'm sorry, I can't, I can't –" Her ladle flies out of her hand onto the ground at my feet and she goes to pick it up.

Seeing her bent in front of me makes me lose my rhythm and the beat turns to cacophony. I imagine her dropping to her knees and tossing her mane of dark brown hair back as she pulls down the waistband on my sweatpants. How she would tease my cock with her tongue until she enveloped it in her plush pink lips. The *sounds* she would make as she sucked and teased me. I don't know if I'd be able to last very long if –

"What's all this?"

I drop the spoons and turn to find my mother in the doorway to the kitchen. That's one way to destroy a fantasy. "Mom! What are you doing home so early?"

"I had a doctor's appointment, so I thought I'd take a half-day," Mom replies.

Jenna pops up. "Hi, Linda!"

"Oh! Jenna! I didn't see you there," Mom says, her eyes wide in surprise.

I turn red as a tomato.

"Chase was just showing me his skills," Jenna chirps. "I'm sorry, I'll clean all this up – "

"No, no, this is great!" she grins and comes over to me, wrapping her arm around my waist. "Reminds me of when he was just a baby."

"*Mom...*" For Christ's sake, I'm a grown man, I don't need to be mortified like a twelve-year-old.

Jenna interrupts. "I was just stopping by to make sure Chase had his lunch, and we got a little off track."

"We're so lucky to have you, aren't we, Chase?" Mom squeezes my ribs and looks up at me.

I stare at Jenna and hope my face isn't betraying what I'm feeling inside. Her pretty eyes flicker in mine. I smile at her. "Yeah. Really lucky."

6

———

JENNA

"I want you so bad."

His voice is ragged in my ear. I've got my hands poised on my binoculars, but I'm not seeing anything through them. I'm too focused on his hand on my collarbone and the way he's pulling me into him. I can feel his hardness against my back.

"Jenna..."

Chase bends his lips toward my chin and begins a trail of kisses up my jawbone. I drop the binoculars when his free hand pushes open the button on my jeans and his fingers dip inside.

I try to moan; nothing comes out.

*Ah, fuck. It's a dream.*

I ride out the dream which becomes a haphazard mess until I wake up. It's only six in the morning, but I can't fall back asleep. I drag myself out of bed, pull on some yoga pants and a sports bra, and go for a morning run. I start off my run jogging past the MacAllistair home. Dan is already up, shuffling away in the kitchen, making probably a breakfast with eighteen eggs or something ridiculous. He sees me and gives me a tight wave and smile.

I wave back sheepishly and take off down the street.

This is not the first time I've had a dream about Chase. It makes sense considering I've been seeing him nearly every weekday for the past month. But I can't help feeling like my brain is betraying me when I have made it painfully clear that Chase is nothing more than a friend, can *be nothing more than a friend.*

It's getting harder to ignore how I feel about him when we spend so much time together.

It doesn't help that my summer basically consists of morning runs, family dinners, and visits with Chase. It's distracted me enough that I've stopped my job search altogether. When Dad asks me how it's going, I just lie and say, "Same old, same old." It'd be impossible to explain that all my time has been taken up by my best friend's older brother.

Not that Rachel ever mentioned it, but the fact that he is her much older brother has made my attraction to Chase difficult from day one. And once he started showing up in my dreams, I could barely look at her. The day after the first dream, we took a drive out to the beach with some of our high school friends and I was silent the entire car ride until she tossed a White Claw into my lap and said, "Loosen up, Jens."

I got ragingly drunk and was so hungover the next day that I thought I had gotten the stomach flu.

The point is, Chase is consuming me. When I'm not with him, I think about him. When I'm not awake, I dream about him. And when I *am* with him...I want him in a way I've never wanted anyone. It feels, sometimes, like I'm making it up. Imagining the whole thing.

I wonder if he can see it on me when we hang out together. If he can tell I'm looking at him with starry eyes as I admire him for the umpteenth time, whether it's his luscious blond locks or the vascularity of his forearms. He's probably so used to the attention that he can see immediately if a girl wants him. I bet he chuckles to himself, thinking I have some schoolgirl crush.

Chase probably thinks I'm pathetic. Maybe Rachel's right and I should try and get out there and find a boyfriend. Maybe then these feelings would go away.

By the time I get back home, I've been gone nearly an hour. I made it around the whole neighborhood, lost in thought. I get ready for the day, debating if I should cancel my usual lunch with Chase. Of course, I want to see him. But it's getting harder to keep these feelings at bay. I'm drowning in the guilt and embarrassment of it. And I feel like I'm wasting my life being hung up on an older guy I can't even have.

Mid-morning, as I'm going through my usual routine, I peer out the dining room window and see Chase is outside today. He's leaning over the table, looking at a set of playing cards that look to be set up like solitaire. He is focused on the cards, so focused that his eyes pinch at the corners.

Against my better judgment, I open the dining room window and lean out to shout, "Hey, how's the hand?"

Chase looks up at me. I notice his beard has been freshly trimmed and the contours of his face are no longer eaten up by facial hair. His jaw and cheekbones are strong and pronounced. His smile makes me feel like I'm a pleasant surprise. I love that smile. "It sucks. Starting to think the dealer has something against me."

I giggle, "Want me to fight him?"

Chase's eyebrows jump. "I didn't take you for a fighter, Jenna."

I shrug. "In dire circumstances such as these, I'm always willing to throw hands."

Chase laughs and looks back down at the cards. We are both quiet for a moment. He draws his sightline up, toward the bank of trees past his lawn. "Beautiful day."

"Yeah, although it's getting pretty hot out."

Chase concedes with a short nod. "Not too bad in the shade, though. Better than being trapped inside."

I don't know what to say. Chase has been so sensitive to this sense that he's trapped. And I can't blame him. The man's a world traveler, for God's sake. He can be in London one night and LA the next. How is he supposed to settle down at his parents' house for two months?

"You busy?" he continues. "Want to come join me for a game?"

I have to restrain how hard I want to smile. "Sure, give me a few minutes."

"A few minutes" is really only about a minute, the way I scramble to throw on my sandals and rush next door, through the gate, and down the side of the house to the back deck.

"Long time, no see," Chase teases. He's cleared the solitaire spread and is now casually shuffling the cards through his hands.

"What are we playing?" I ask, plopping down across the table from him.

He raises an eyebrow. "Well, what do you want to play?"

"Dealer's choice," I say. "I'm a fast learner."

"Well, I mean...what am I working with here? You a Texas hold'em girl or a 'go fish' girl?"

I scoff. "A 'go fish' girl? Don't *insult* me, Chase."

He flushes around his nose. "Sorry! Sorry, I didn't know!"

"I lived in a dorm my first two years of college. I know how to play more than 'go fish'."

"You a gambler?" Chase asks, cocking his head to the side.

I shake my head. "Not usually."

"You know blackjack?"

I smile slyly to myself. *Do I know blackjack?* Back in the dorms, I was a blackjack *master*. I don't know whether it was luck or strategy; what I do know is that I earned enough drinking money for Rachel and me for a whole semester. "Yeah, I'm familiar."

"Okay," Chase says with a nod. "We'll start with that."

Chase deals us both two cards, one face up and one face down. "No cheating," I say to him admonishingly.

"Oh, I never cheat," he says. "I play cards with too many strangers to cheat."

"You play a lot on the road?"

"All the time. Especially when we're in bumfuck nowhere," Chase says and then smiles like he's got a secret. "And it's a good way to keep ourselves out of trouble. Rather than...you know."

He doesn't have to say it: sex, drugs, rock'n'roll. For some reason, there's a pang in my heart when I think about Chase tumbling into bed with whatever the girl of the night is in whatever city they're in. I shake it off. We both peek at our face-down card. I've got a Jack and a four. Both of hearts, not that it matters. Chase has a nine. "Okay. Hit me."

Chase puts a three down. Seventeen...not bad, but not great. "Stay."

"I stay, too," Chase says.

We flip over our cards. He's got nineteen, so he won this round. He collects the cards. "You want to play through the deck? Whoever gets all the cards wins?"

"You're on."

"Should we make a bet?" he asks, a glint of excitement on his face.

I hum in consideration. "Sure. What do you want to bet?"

Chase looks off into the distance and then says, "How about whoever loses has to surprise the other person with something? Like a gift. Nothing big. Just a small, 'I'm a loser' gift."

I laugh. "Okay. Bet."

In the next round, Chase busts at twenty-three after two hits, and I get the hand at sixteen. "You flew too close to the sun," I tease as he deals out the next hand.

"Yeah, well, the higher the risk, the higher the reward," Chase replies. His icy blue eyes meet mine. "Where's the fun in playing it safe?"

My tongue is frozen. I can't help but feel like he's talking about more than blackjack. We continue the game and, for a while, the power is balanced, back and forth. I'll have to show him what I'm really made of.

I end up winning three rounds in a row, with one of them being a perfect twenty-one. Chase is impressed. "Are you hustling me?"

"Me? A hustler? *Please*," I avoid answering the question with feigned innocence in my words.

He narrows his eyes at me; they're darker now, the intensity bringing out the deeper hues of blue in his irises. I want to look away to avoid falling deeper under his spell but decide to show him I'm a formidable challenger. I'm not scared. "Deal, MacAllistair."

The next several rounds go quickly. I take some risks and lose a couple of hands, but Chase follows suit and suddenly, I've got about three quarters of the deck in my possession.

"You're a hustler, Jenna!" he says in playful frustration, running a hand back through his tangled blond locks.

"I'm not! I'm just lucky, I guess," I reply and then add, "But, in case you're already thinking of gifts, I am very partial to chocolate."

Chase puts his tongue in the corner of his mouth and shakes his head. I don't think he's sure he believes me, but it's too much fun to mess with his head. He's playing hard and he's playing fast. We're both saying "Hit" without thinking too long. My head is swimming with simple math. I no longer care if I win or not, all I care about is watching him and how he plays the game.

The final hand, all I've got is a three and an ace. Four or fourteen, depending on if I play the ace low or high. Chase has a seven and decided to hold his hand where it is. "Hit me," I say.

Chase chews on the inside of his lip. His eyelids are low, laser-focused on trying to read my face. He takes a card and gently unfurls it onto my deck. A five. "What the hell," I say and smile playfully. "Hit me again."

"Again?" Chase asks like I'm crazy.

I lean forward so we're closer to each other. "Again," I say, taunting him with the way my lips move around the word.

Chase hesitates, captured by my stare. He takes one of the last cards and puts it face up on my deck. A two. Perfect twenty-one. I can't help but grin. "Hold."

I see his Adam's apple bob as he swallows. He sheepishly flips over his cards. A seven and a nine. Sixteen.

"Not bad..."

"But..." Chase says, knowing I'm about to beat him.

I flip over my card. "Read it and weep, MacAllistair. A perfect twenty—"

I'm not able to get the word out before he kisses me. *Oh my god, he's kissing me?!* He's fucking kissing me. And this time, I'm not dreaming. His wide hands capture the sides of my face. I know that if this stupid table weren't in the way, he'd have me pulled tight against his chest.

Chase's lips are soft and lush, but the way he rolls his tongue around my mouth is rough and *needy*. I know I should pull away. I just can't. I lean further into it, looping my arms around his neck. We are both so desperate; each time our lips part one of us lets out a ragged breath or whimper.

My head is swimming. I can't even believe this is happening. It feels so good and right. My entire body lights up like a Christmas tree, all my nerves on fire. The day is hot, pleasant in the shade, but now it's even hotter. I feel like I'm working up a sweat just from the way his lips are working against mine.

"Jenna..." he murmurs against my lips and moves one of his hands from my face to my waist. His fingers bend against the curve of my spine, brushing up against the top of my ass.

My heart is beating a mile a minute. I want to scramble over the table into his lap and let him take me in a way no one has before.

But suddenly, my phone rings, blaring loud and scaring the shit out of me. I leap back from Chase and fall on my ass, catching myself with my hands. We stare at one another. The space between us filled by the stupid ringtone. I don't even remember having the blasted ringer on.

Chase's mouth hangs open, spit dewy on his lips. His forehead pinches at the center as if he's confused by what just happened. As if he wasn't even in control of what came over him.

I remember I actually have to *pick up* my phone when it rings. I look at the screen and swallow. "It's Rachel." I try to read in his eyes if he thinks I should pick it up. Chase is of no help now, though. He's been rendered beyond speechless.

I feel like if I don't pick up it will be suspicious. I press the green circular button and put the phone to my ear. "What's up, Rach?"

"Hey! I'm out of class early today. You want to come pick me up and we can go get lunch together? My treat!" Rachel's voice bubbles joyfully out of the speaker.

Chase's eyes are trained on me. I will myself not to look at him. "Sounds fun! Sounds great. Let me grab my car and I'll be over in like 20. Sound good?"

"Sounds perfect. See you then."

I hang up the phone and stare at the ground. There's a knot in the wooden deck and I trace the circular pattern with my eyes.

"I'm sorry," Chase's voice creaks out of him.

"It's okay."

"No, I...don't know what came over me."

I can hear the regret in his voice. My heart breaks. I bite the inside of my cheek to keep from crying.

"Forget it happened, okay?" he says, a half-hearted laugh under his words. "The meds are getting to me."

"Right, totally," I reply, but my words are cut with

disappointment. I get to my feet and take a step back, awkwardly pointing toward my house. "I should go."

Chase nods. "Totally."

"But...I'll see you." I'm holding my jaw so tensely that the whole front of my neck hurts. I hope I never see him again and wish I could disappear off the face of the earth.

He doesn't respond right away, so I take that as my cue to leave. But just as I start down the steps of the deck, he calls my name. "Jenna."

My whole body melts at the way my name fits in his mouth and how it resounds in his chest. I turn back, trying to give him one more smile.

"You beat me," Chase says. "Fair and square."

I laugh, although it comes out like a dying animal. "I hustled you, Chase."

"Oh, I know," he replies.

We are both quiet, stuck in a longing gaze. At least, I long for him. Long to walk right back over and kiss him again and make him *not* regret it. I long to give myself over to him and let him know that I want to say "fuck it" to everything and let him have me. I've never felt this way about anyone, ever. Not even my high school boyfriend whose name I wore on a gold necklace for two years.

But in his eyes, I see it. The cracks in his cool, suave façade. *We can't.*

And he's right.

I can't face him any longer. Don't know if I can ever face him again. I walk as fast as I can without running back to my house, grab my car keys off the counter, and jump into the car. As I drive, the radio blares, and I'm met with the unwelcome sound of a radio announcer rambling, "Next, our hometown heroes, Soul Sounds with 'Visitor'."

I swallow and clutch the steering wheel tighter.

*Wandering, without a home*
*Directionless and searching*
*The roads look the same wherever you go*
*But when I find her, I'll be certain.*

Fuck this. I turn off the radio and suddenly, I'm angry. I'm angry because Chase MacAllistair isn't just my best friend's brother, but he's a famous musician and he's used to getting what he wants and doing what he wants without consequences. A "hometown hero." And who am I? Just a girl who loves birds who can't find a job. How pathetic. How *embarrassing*. And he just fucking kissed me, and now I'm left to deal with it.

As if I don't have enough on my mind.

By the time I pull up to the business school, my anger has completely receded. In its place, is the echo of the kiss on my lips and blood coursing through my body. And all that does is make me sad knowing that I can never, never, *never* kiss Chase again.

Rachel appears at the passenger door and knocks on the window, waving wildly, with a big grin.

I sigh and unlock the door.

"Hey, queen!" Rachel greets me enthusiastically and climbs into the car. "I don't know about you, but I'm feeling tacos. I've been craving those babies like crazy. Is that okay?"

I can't look at her, staring out ahead of me through the windshield. "Sounds fine."

"Unless you wanted something else. I'm flexible," she says in a sing-song tone.

"Tacos...is good," I say with a half-hearted smile.

Rachel frowns and her lips droop. "Jens? Are you okay?"

I start to nod, but I've never been good at keeping my

feelings in. My face breaks and suddenly tears are streaming down my face. Rachel throws her arms around me and holds me, which makes me cry harder.

"Oh my god, baby, what's wrong?" she asks, stroking my back.

I can't respond. I can't tell her what happened. She'll be furious.

"Is it the job thing?"

I nod into her chest.

"Aw. It's okay, Jens. Really. You'll find something. And it'll be perfect. Fuck all those people who aren't giving you the time of day. They don't know what they're missing."

I sigh. If this is the worst lie I tell in my life, then I think I'll be okay. But Rachel cannot, under any circumstances, know that I've just kissed her big brother.

That would ruin everything.

## 7

## CHASE

"Go long!" Dan shouts across the yard.

"Fuck off!" I shout back. I've propped myself up with my crutches at one end of the backyard to pass the football back and forth with Dan. It's a sad excuse for a game of catch, but it's the best I can do. The twilight hours have brought a nice breeze, cooling off an extra hot day which kept me inside most of it.

Dan tosses the football and I catch it seamlessly. It's been a nice weekend. Lots of family time. Tonight, we had a classic barbecue outside with hotdogs and hamburgers. Mom made her infamous Jell-O salad (which shouldn't be as good as it is). Mom and Dad are cleaning up the remnants of our dinner from the deck table while us kids "play" on the lawn. Like old times, I guess. But in the old times, I didn't have so much on my mind. I wasn't worried about what would happen tomorrow in the way I am now.

I throw the football back and Dan leaps up to get it. "Sorry!" I shout back. I've never been good with the football thing. Clearly, Dan got all those genes. And it suits him. He really embraces the whole lifestyle. He's bulky and tall and keeps his blonde hair cropped short.

I look briefly at Rachel who is painting her toenails while sitting on the steps down from the deck. She's been in all weekend with no plans with friends which is unusual for her. "You're stuck with me, Chasey!" she chirped Saturday morning when she plopped down on the couch next to me.

I've screwed it all up, I really have. Not only did I kiss Jenna, who is absolutely, totally off-limits, but now I've tainted my relationship with my sister because every time I look at her, all I can think about is...Jenna.

From Rachel, my eyes travel over to the house next door. One that isn't entirely unlike ours with its white siding and large gray roof. But the window frames are painted cornflower blue and there seem to be more windows. I can see Jenna's room from here. I'd be lying if I said I hadn't spent time trying to figure out which window was hers. After all, what else am I supposed to do with all this time? And to be fair, it wasn't hard to figure out because her curtains are light purple with moons and stars all over them, no doubt a holdover from when she was a little girl.

*She's still a little girl...*

Jenna appears at the window, as if I've conjured her there just by staring too long. She's got her binoculars in hand and she's peering out at the trees behind the house to watch the nest. And framed there, between the purple curtains, all I see is a beautiful young woman with her dark hair pinned back on her head. Like a goddamn Renaissance painting, or –

My daydreaming is interrupted when I'm thwacked with the football right to my face. My nose immediately throbs. I put my hand to it to make sure I'm not bleeding.

"Jesus Christ, Dan!" Rachel shouts and rushes over to me. "He's already injured!"

"It's not my fault he wasn't paying attention!" Dan yells back gruffly.

I pull my hand away. No blood. "It's fine, guys. But maybe I should call it quits. Clearly, I'm not…" I trail off as I look back up at Jenna's room. She's looking out her window at us, drawn to the commotion. As soon as our eyes meet, I feel like I want to burst into a million pieces out of embarrassment.

Jenna raises her hand and gives me a small wave. I smile back. And while I'm still filled with dread and embarrassment for what happened, I remember something.

I still owe her for beating my ass at blackjack.

"What do you need a drone for?" Jay asks as I open the shopping bag.

"It's a gift," I answer. "Thanks for bringing this over, man, I owe you." Jay was kind enough to run to Best Buy and get me a drone. For Jenna.

Jay frowns, his lips curling in confusion. "Whose birthday is it?"

"Not a birthday. I lost a bet."

"To whom?"

"Does it matter?"

His eyes narrow. "You're being avoidant. And suspicious."

I roll my eyes and lean against the kitchen counter. "For our neighbor. She's a birdwatcher."

Jay's face softens. "Ohhh…that nice old lady across the street? Why were you betting with her?"

"Not Mrs. Cartwright, Jay," I say more annoyedly than I'd like. "Rachel's friend next door."

His navy eyes widen. "Rachel's friend? The pretty one?"

"*Jay*," I say as a warning. A spark of jealousy creeps inside me.

"I just never would have pegged her as a birdwatcher," he says, shrugging. "So what was the bet?"

"We were playing blackjack."

Jay's lips curl in a sly smile.

"What?"

"You know what."

"No, I don't."

Jay wanders over to the fridge, opens it, and pulls out some grapes from a bag. My home has always been his and vice versa, but at this moment, I want him to leave before he starts prodding me about things I don't want to talk about. "Playing cards...making bets...sounds like flirting."

"Oh *please*. That's insane."

"You're getting defensive," Jay says with a mouthful of grape.

"Don't talk with your mouth full," I reply bitterly.

Jay sighs, finishes chewing, and swallows. "And now you're changing the subject."

"We've been hanging out a little bit. That's all," I say, cotton-mouthed from lying. "We made a bet over blackjack, I lost. I owe her."

"You owe her a *drone*?"

I'm flustered now. "Look, man, you wouldn't get it, okay? Just – thank you so much for dropping this off and get the fuck out of my house."

Despite all his teasing, Jay is beaming. "Aww...Chase. You've got a crush."

"I *do not.*"

"Do too!"

"Do not!"

"Do too! And it's okay! It's natural!"

I can't keep it in any longer. "Listen to me, Jay. It's not and will never be a thing. So, please, shut the fuck up about it and forget that – "

"Sorry to interrupt."

I jump at the sound of Jenna's voice and turn as quickly as I can, given the condition of my leg, toward the doorway of the kitchen. There she is. Looking as beautiful as…I wave the thought away. "Hi, Jenna," I say with a pitiful amount of awkwardness in my voice.

"Hi," she says back. We both stare at each other, the kiss we shared a few days ago unspoken, but very much present in the energy between us. Jenna bites her lip and raises her eyebrows as if daring me to say something about it.

"Well, hey there," Jay suddenly interrupts, brushing past me toward Jenna. "I'm Jay. We met briefly when – "

She smiles at him. "Yeah, I remember you. It's good to see you."

"You too," Jay replies. He gives a look to me over his shoulder and mouths, *Come on, man.*

"I can go if y'all have plans, sorry to –"

Jay interrupts eagerly, "No! Nothing to be sorry about. I was actually, conveniently, just leaving." He grabs my hand and shakes it heartily. "Good to see you, man. Rest that leg, alright? We need you on that bass pedal."

I bite my tongue to keep from cursing him out. "Thanks for stopping by, Jay."

"Oh, my pleasure, my pleasure." He's laying it on so thick it feels almost satirical. "Nice to see you again, Jenna."

"You too," Jenna replies.

Jay scrambles out of the room like a fucking Loony Tune. Both Jenna and I are silent until the front door slams. And then after that too. It's impossible to know where to start. I try to read her expression, but it's extremely calm. Soft. She's painted her lips with a peachy gloss, making them look big and full. The longer I look, the more I think about kissing them again and wish I could feel them on every square inch of my body.

"What's that for?" Jenna asks suddenly in the silence. She's pointing at the drone on the kitchen island, still in the box.

I hobble back over to it and pick it up. "It's your surprise. For beating me."

Jenna's eyebrows jump. "Oh my god, Chase."

"Because you did beat me," I go on. "Fair and square."

"Yeah, but..." Jenna crosses her arms under her breasts nervously. I can't help but look at how their fullness settles into the cradle of her arms. "That's not like a *little* surprise. That's like a big surprise."

I shrug. "Well, a bet's a bet." I hold the box out to her. "It's yours."

She doesn't uncross her arms; I feel like I've done something wrong, like I've made everything worse. *Shit.*

"I thought you could use it to get a good look at the nest."

Jenna squinches her lips to the side and draws her hazel eyes up to mine. I've never noticed how deep and dark they can feel. I've always been compelled by the light splashes of green and gold. Now, I feel totally lost. She takes the box gingerly from me. "That was really nice of you, Chase."

"Nah. Just..."

"Really thoughtful," Jenna reaffirms. A soft smile

appears on her lips. I feel like I can breathe again. "Should we try it out?"

My stomach drops. I hadn't expected her to use it while she was here. Then again, I hadn't totally expected her to show up today anyway. "Y-yeah. Yeah, let's do it."

We go out onto the deck. I have to rest on the deck sofa. My leg's been killing me. It gets worse when I'm stressed or upset, I've noticed. Jenna unboxes the drone carefully, and we look through the instructions. "This looks...complicated," she says unsurely.

"It can't be that hard, can it?"

Oh, but it can. Jenna sets the drone out on the lawn and we have several false starts where it ends up going sideways into the backyard of her house. We laugh a lot through the frustration and I almost forget that things are a bit off between us. Almost. Except when she's tossing her hair over her shoulder and bending over to reset the drone, showing off her curves through her tight jean shorts. The flank of her thigh looks like the perfect place to rest my cheek.

"Okay!" she announces. "You ready?"

I nod and give her a thumbs up. *God, I'm such a dork.*

Jenna starts the drone and maneuvers it off the ground. For the first time, it actually goes straight into the hair and hovers elegantly over the yard. She looks back at me with a grin, so girlish and sweet.

The drone hovers out into the trees; she navigates the branches with precision and ease. "Let's see...almost..." she mutters to herself, looking at the screen attached to the remote. "Oh. Oh! Chase! I found them! One of them has already hatched!"

She bounds excitedly up the deck, her eyes glued to the screen. "Oh my gosh, one of them's already –" She shoves the controller toward me, beaming with the splendor of the sun. "Look!"

I take the controller from her, but I don't care. I've already got what I wanted from this. Her smile, her joy... maybe I've made things a bit better. Maybe we can move past this. I look down at the screen and, sure enough, there are four eggs in the nest, one already cracked open with a gremlin-looking baby bird straining its neck toward the camera.

Jenna sits on the couch next to me and leans over to get a better look at the screen. I can smell her angelic perfume with her so close. I wish I could bury my nose in her hair. She points at the image. "He must be confused by the drone, probably thinks it's his mom or something."

"The classic drone or mom conundrum," I murmur wryly.

Jenna giggles. The joy on her face is unfettered. "Thank you, Chase. This is just...this is the best." She moves closer to me, hesitating briefly, and then, retreats. Like she was going to give me a hug or something. "I can't thank you enough."

She explores with the drone for another half hour before she leaves. "I'll see you tomorrow," she says before she goes.

I'm thinking about her hesitation hours after she's left. It keeps me awake late into the night. I wish she hadn't hesitated. I wish she had reached out and wrapped her arms around me. That would have been foolish, though.

Because if Jenna had fallen into my arms, I know there's no way I would have ever let her go.

## 8

## JENNA

I'm glad we can move past the kiss. I had debated if I should go back yesterday to see Chase, but I'm really glad I did, drone or no drone.

He's an *adult*. Not like these *boys* I go to college with, who kiss you at a thirsty Thursday party and then act like you don't exist when you see them in the dining hall. No. Chase can be mature about it. And I'm grateful I don't have to lose his friendship since we...

Anyway. Today, I'm going over with a gift in return. It's not much, nothing like a drone. But I thought some iced lemon cookies would be a nice treat to brighten his spirits. It's an old family recipe; my mom and I made them last night and juiced more lemons than I could count for the batch. The powdered sugar for the icing got everywhere and we woke Dad up by vacuuming the kitchen late at night.

I let myself in the usual way, with less trepidation than I had yesterday. Now that Chase has gotten the hang of his crutches and his leg is feeling better, he's usually not on the couch in the living room. Sometimes, he's already in the kitchen or out on the deck. On a couple of occasions, he was in his room which is down the hall, past the staircase, tucked away and small. He sleeps in an XL twin bed like he's in a dorm room, and when I saw it, he immediately went red in the face and said, "I don't sleep in a twin bed anymore."

Obviously, Chase.

Today, though...no Chase. Not in the living room, not in the kitchen, not on the deck, not even in his bedroom, or the bathroom (which I nervously peer into after knocking). I go back to the living room and call out his name. No answer. I catch sight of a half-full bottle of vodka on the table. I feel my eyes widen and cheeks tighten. He couldn't have...are things really that bad? That he's so upset he now feels like he has to start drinking in the middle of the day?

From upstairs comes a loud clunking sound like something's fallen on the ground and someone's muffled voice.

"For fuck's sake..." I mutter and put the cookies on the coffee table.

If this idiot went upstairs, I don't know what I'll do. I climb the staircase, calling, "Chase! Chaaaase!"

"In here!" he calls back.

I go down the hall to Mr. MacAllistair's office and find Chase trying to bend over to pick up one of his crutches. "What the hell are you doing up here?"

"I needed a..." he pants as he strains for the crutch. "I needed a pen."

I snatch the crutch off the ground and hold it up for him.

"Hey! I almost had it."

"Don't be a martyr," I snort. "There are pens downstairs!"

Chase takes the crutch with playful disdain and shakes

his head. "There aren't. There's a pen deficit. A shortage. A famine."

"It can't be a famine unless you eat them."

"I have an ink problem, please don't tell my family," he begs melodramatically.

I remember the bottle of alcohol on the table. Chase definitely seems way too lucid and steady to be drunk, although I guess I can't be sure. Lots of musicians are addicts and probably function just fine with half a bottle of vodka in their system. "What's with the vodka downstairs?" I ask.

Chase smiles crookedly and narrows his eyes. "Follow me."

We go back down the stairs, me spotting Chase the whole way while he waves me off again and again.

"I'm fine, I'm fine, Jenna!"

Back in the living room, Chase goes to the bottle of vodka and picks up a pile of small papers with jagged edges I hadn't noticed there before. "I made a card game!" he announces proudly.

"Aha..." I nod, thinking I know what he's up to. "You want a second chance to beat me?"

"No, no, not at all," Chase says, almost smug. "You beat me, fair and square. I'm a big enough man to accept that."

I have to bite the inside of my cheek at the notion of him being a "big enough man". My mind immediately goes to what's between his legs. *Get your mind out of the gutter, Jenna.*

"I thought we'd play a different sort of game. A drinking game."

I chuckle. "It's like...eleven in the morning."

"So?"

"We're not all rockstars, Chase."

Chase sighs and looks away, trying not to be annoyed with me. "I'm not a *rockstar*."

"You're on the radio! You're literally – "

"Then step into my world for a second and drink at eleven in the morning, Jenna!" Chase cries out with a bold grin. "Where's the harm?"

Where *is* the harm? It's a good question. As far as drinking at eleven am, I guess I don't have much else to do the rest of the day. I was going to run to Target in the afternoon...that was about it. "Okay. Fine. I'll take a walk on the wild side."

"Well, if you're going to do that, start by not saying 'walk on the wild side'," Chase mocks, head bobbling on his neck.

"Shut up, don't be an ass," I tut.

"Okay, you sit over there and I'll sit here and –" Chase gestures to either end of the couch but stops short when his eyes land on the cookies. "Did you bring these?"

I bashfully reach for the container of cookies and open it. "Uh, yeah, they're lemon cookies. My mom and I made them, and I thought you might – "I crack open the container and the scent of lemon immediately permeates the room.

"Perfect, it can be like a chaser," Chase grins. "Although not a bad way to start." He takes a cookie out of the container and shoves most of it in his mouth. "Oh, fuck," he says, covering his mouth with his hand. "This is so good." He reaches for another one before the first is finished, but I snap the lid shut.

"Uh, uh, uh," I admonish. "We're saving them for the game. Now. Tell me the rules."

Chase and I post up on either side of the couch, his leg up extended on the ottoman and me folded up crisscross with a pillow in my lap, almost protectively. He explains the game while shuffling the makeshift cards through his hands. "It's a bit like 'Never Have I Ever' except it's more like 'Have You Ever?'. Rules are simple. You pick up a card, ask the other player the question, and if they answer 'no'..." Chase grabs the bottle of vodka and tosses it toward me. I catch it with ease. "You gotta take a shot."

"Straight from the bottle?"

"That's how us rockers do it..." he says, rolling his eyes. "Ready?"

Chase holds out the cards to me, but I'm still skeptical. I raise an eyebrow at him quizzically. "This doesn't seem fair. Since you wrote all the cards. How do I know they're not all like 'Have you ever ridden a motorcycle down the hallway of a hotel?'"

"First of all, the days of that kind of behavior are long gone with Led Zeppelin," he says, wagging his finger at me. "And second of all, I think you'll find I was fair. One of the cards is, 'Have you ever spent a day birdwatching?' So, don't worry, they're tailored to you." Chase holds out the deck of cards to me. "Ladies first."

I reluctantly take a card and narrow my eyes at him. "You just want to see me drunk, don't you?"

"Hey, I know the kinds of parties you and Rachel go to. They sound crazy."

"I'm usually the designated driver," I murmur with a flick of my hair over my shoulder and then look down at the card. "Have you ever been blackout drunk?"

Chase rolls his eyes. "Yeah. Obviously."

I shrug. "Okay. My turn."

Chase takes a card from his deck. "Have you ever skinny dipped?" His eyes shoot up to mine apologetically. "*Okay*, I didn't expect it to start so hard so fast, I promise, but – "

"Yes," I answer plainly, holding the bottle of vodka out to him.

Chase's eyes widen like big pools of water and his cheeks sink in. "I'm sorry?"

"The answer is yes, now *your turn.*"

"Woah, woah, woah, you can't just –" Chase is talking faster than his brain can comprehend this information and it's really charming that the guy who always knows the right thing to say is babbling like a baby. "Start from the beginning."

"It's, like, not an interesting story."

"Um. Yeah, it is."

We stare at each other. I can't help but wonder if the story is so interesting because he's pictured me naked before. I can't really judge him for that since I've definitely tried to imagine what his chest looks like under his tight tank tops. "Um...it was senior week. In high school. And basically, there's this list of challenges to complete hosted by the student government, and whoever wins gets an all-expense paid trip to Splashtown, so me and Rachel and Dan and a couple others formed a group and we had to get all these things done and – "

"Student government told you to *skinny dip?*" Chase asked incredulously.

"Well...there were the things that they advertised as part of the challenge. Like wear colorful wigs to school or make a music video with one of the teachers...and then there were the sort of secret challenges. It basically got you extra points and so...we..." I feel my mouth growing hot. The story is funny, but it's not like a sexy spring break thing like I think Chase is looking for.

Chase's shock wears away and he grins at me. "Right on."

I take the next card. "Have you been to college?"

He sighs. "See, I told you I catered it to you!"

"Take a drink, MacAllistair." Chase swigs the vodka like a pro, not even flinching as he swallows. I sympathetically stick out my tongue. "Meh...it's not even flavored."

"Oh, Jenna...you're so young," he laughs. "That shit gives me headaches."

I know that his age really puts a sort of barrier between us, but I love that he's older than me. It doesn't feel patronizing. It just feels like we can reveal life to each other in a different way. I'm younger, in college, pursuing a sensible degree. He's older, a musician, always on the road, onto the next thing.

Some say opposites attract, don't they?

"Have you ever sung in front of people?" Chase asks from a card, a smirk on his face.

I roll my eyes. "Bottle, please."

Chase tosses it over and I take a sip. I am not as graceful in swallowing as he is and cough as soon as the heat makes its way to the base of my throat. "*Blaaaarghh,*" I wheeze.

"Aw. You'll get better, Jens, I promise."

I hesitate before taking another card. Rachel calls me Jens. Dan *sometimes* calls me Jens. Chase calls me Jens now? I'll let it slide. "Okay, your turn."

WE'VE BEEN GOING BACK AND FORTH FOR A WHILE. I'VE had way more vodka than a person should have in one sitting, especially in the middle of the day. My head is swimming and my face is hot. But *what the hell,* I'm having a blast. Chase and I have been trading life stories back and forth, like the time he was cornered in a venue dressing room by Madonna and how I got locked in the school library during midterms last year.

"Have you ever broken a bone?" I read off a card and look at Chase with a silly smile.

"Like this fracture?" He points at his leg.

I gape at him feigning surprise. "You're in a cast!"

And I have the x-rays to prove it." He smiles smugly.

"Fine!" I huff, extending my legs down the couch and poking him with my toes. "Read the next card."

Chase gives me a shit-eating grin; he's the only person that can make a face like that and still be so handsome. *Shit.* The vodka is hitting me hard. Suddenly, kissing him doesn't seem like the *biggest* thing I could do wrong in the world. The worst thing I could do is probably murder...or tax fraud...or –

"Have you ever had sex in public?"

I feel as though I've run directly into a brick wall when he asks that question, and I'm so stunned, my answer comes out of me in a galumphing laugh, "Um, *no.* I've never had sex *at all*, let alone in public." I laugh at the ludicrousness of the question and realize after a minute that I'm laughing by myself.

Chase is looking at me with shock and curiosity. I can't tell if he's judging me or trying to study me like a bug. Whatever it is, I don't like it.

"Okay, that's enough," I mutter and reach for the vodka bottle.

"Sorry, I don't mean to stare or – "

"Yeah, well, you were anyway," I say coldly before taking a swig of vodka.

"Sorry," Chase says. His words have started softening around the edges, not quite slurring, but definitely tinged with the effects of alcohol. "Are you...saving it for marriage, or – "

"Dude, come on."

He holds his hands up defensively. "Sorry, is that a bad question?"

"Yeah, because it's none of your business," I shoot back.

"You're right. You're totally right. I'm sorry I asked."

We sit in silence. I stare at the pile of cards in his hand and then look at the front door. It'd make things worse if I just got up and left, but my skin is crawling thinking about having to continue this conversation. "It's not – I'm not saving myself for marriage."

"It'd be fine if you were, like power to you if it's – "

"Well, I'm not."

"Okay. Okay..." Chase says, nervously swallowing. "It's just hard to believe. That you haven't."

I look at him with fire in my eyes, not meaning to look as angry as I probably do. "What's that supposed to mean?"

He sits up as best he can. "Jenna, I mean...I don't know. You're..."

"Are all college girls just supposed to be fucking around all the time? Is that what you think of me?"

Chase's eyes are wide now. "No, holy crap! That's not what I said!"

"Then, why are you surprised? What's the big deal? It's just sex."

"I'm just surprised because you're gorgeous and amazing to be around, so it's hard for me to believe that guys aren't falling at your feet all the fucking time, so..." Chase replies, frustration tinging his voice.

Whether or not he realizes what he's said, I don't care. My heart bunches up in my mouth. *Gorgeous...amazing...* It's not just nice to be described that way. It's nice to be described that way by *him*. "I'm just waiting for the right person," I say quietly.

"Well, good. You should," he says. "You deserve for it to be perfect because you're...yeah."

I smile at him tenderly. Though my mind is clouded with alcohol, I feel so much clarity in this moment.

"God. Can we just forget I said anything and just move on? I think I'm drunk," Chase groans and runs his hands over his face.

But I don't want to forget. I don't want to move on. I don't care what stands in my way. I want Chase MacAllistair. I want him with every fiber of my being. So, when Chase turns back to me with a crinkling smile, saying, "Man, I really am getting old," I lunge for him, engulf his face in my hands and press my lips to his in a hungry kiss.

Chase hums in surprise against my lips but quickly settles into it, his hands resting against my waist. I run my hands through his blond hair, relish in his beard bristling against my face, and devour him with my lips. Our tongues clash and flip with more grace now than the first time we kissed; clearly, our bodies haven't forgotten what that felt like.

Chase breaks the seal of our kiss, but he can't go far, only an inch. "Jenna," he says gruffly. "We can't."

"I know," I reply and kiss him again.

He melts beneath me, clutches at my waist, runs a hand up my back. I swing my leg over his lap, careful with his leg, and straddle his hips. When our lips break, he tries to protest again, "Someone could walk in."

"I don't care."

"Oh god."

We return to the dance of our lips and tongues. I readjust his hand down from my waist to my ass. "Touch me," I say with a heaving breath before pushing my face down into his neck.

Chase's broad hand stretches out against the roundness of my ass, sending a wave of delight coursing through my body, starting in my pelvis. "Oh my god, Jenna..." he moans.

As I trail kisses down his neck, I inhale his musk. Freshly showered, clean, the trace of beard oil, maybe. Something like bergamot.

His hands tighten on my ass, pull me into his pelvis, and that's when I feel him. Hard. Right there under me. So hard. I lift my head and look into his eyes, hoping not to betray my uneasiness. Chase lessens the intensity of his grasp, but I can't ignore how wide his pupils have gotten. "I'm sorry," he says.

"It's okay," I reply. I put a hand up against his chest and feel his heart racing through his bulging pectorals. "You can't really help it."

Chase laughs raggedly and closes his eyes. "Uh, no. It's hard to help, especially with a beautiful girl on my lap."

I smile and give him another small kiss on the lips, chaste this time. "I want it to be you," I whisper. "I want it to be you, Chase."

An air of fear passes over his face. I know it can't be because he's scared of *it*, of... sex. He's had a lot of it from what I've heard and I'm sure he's played down how loose and free he really is on the road. "Jenna, listen, you should wait. For someone who is younger, or, at the very least, has a good leg."

"I don't care about your leg," I say, nestling tighter against his pelvis.

Chase takes in a tight breath. "Yes, but...we shouldn't. With Rachel and Dan and – "

"Fuck them!" I say with a smile on my face, which

immediately gets a bit warmer with my brazenness. "I don't care who you're related to or how old you are or anything. I want you, Chase."

His forehead pinches at the center as he takes in what I've said.

"Don't you want me?" Fear suddenly fills me at the thought that he might find me lacking somehow.

Chase's face relaxes. He smiles and his eyes glaze with lust. "Of course, I do."

I give him another kiss and then say the words he's been waiting for: "Then fuck me."

Chase's blue eyes darken even more than I thought possible. Abruptly, his hesitancy disappears. He pulls me back toward him and kisses me again, harder, needier than before.

Our pelvises begin to rock into one another, through our clothes. Each nudge of his cock against my groin shoots a tickle of pleasure through me. He's big. I can tell even now. And I'm not scared at the prospect of taking him. I'm thrilled.

Chase reaches for the tie on my halter top and asks, "Is this okay?"

"Yeah, yes," I nod heavily.

He pulls on the bow and the fabric tumbles down, revealing my breasts to the air. My nipples immediately harden. Chase admires the view with his jaw hanging open. "Fuck, Jenna..." he mutters before pressing his lips to one of my nipples.

I watch as he indulges, caressing them in his wide hands, lapping at them with his tongue. I feel myself getting wetter. As if he knows, Chase raises his gaze back up to me, mouth still wrapped around my nipple. Fuck, he's hot. He's so hot. I didn't think a guy as hot as Chase would ever be into me, but here he is, with my breasts in his hands. Worshipping me.

I reach down for the hem of his tank top and pull it up. His abs are tight, a trail of hair leading down his belly into his jeans. Chase pulls the tank top the rest of the way up his chest and over his head. The plane of his torso is a fucking marvel. Hair sprinkles his chest, accenting the subtle definition of his muscles. "Only fair," he says with a small shrug.

I laugh and run my arms down his biceps. They feel even better than I imagined.

Chase touches the button of my shorts. "You tell me if it's too much. I'll stop."

I nod but don't say anything. I'm not going to tell him to stop.

Chase undoes my shorts, parts them, and threads his fingers inside, pushing my panties aside and brushing up against my wet center. I shudder.

"Fuck, you're so wet," he murmurs. Chase curls his fingers slightly until they dip inside me.

I take in a deep breath. I've been touched and played with before. But never by someone I really, truly wanted. Someone I wanted inside me.

Chase pumps his fingers inside me, stretching me, preparing me. "Feels so good...can't wait to be inside you..."

I ride his fingers for a few minutes, my head lolling to the side. Warmth pools out in my belly.

Chase withdraws his hand suddenly and grabs me by the shoulders. "Stop, stop."

"What? What is it?"

"Shhh..." he urgently shushes, looking over my shoulder.

I follow his gaze toward the front door, and we wait in silence.

"Thought I heard someone," Chase says.

We lie in wait for another minute. My pulse, which had been raging, settles. I suddenly become upsettingly aware of my surroundings. I'm preparing to fuck my best friend's brother in her living room, the living room I've been playing in since I was just a toddler.

Something about it...is so fucked up...and so exciting at the same time.

"I think it was just my imagination," Chase says sheepishly.

I turn back to him and smile. "Are you comfortable?"

Chase lifts his good leg off the ottoman and puts his foot flat on the floor. "Better now. Leverage."

"Leverage," I repeat with a laugh in my voice. "I see..."

Chase inclines his head back on the couch. "Come here."

I drift back into his orbit. Chase wraps his hand around the back of my head and kisses me viciously, picking up right where we left off. We both reach down between us to pull down on the band of his track pants and move my shorts further down my legs.

"Oh my god, Jenna," Chase says breathlessly against my mouth. "I want you so bad."

"You can have me," I say back.

Chase growls at the thought of having me. I imagine if he could, he'd pin me down on the couch and fuck me raw and hard. Instead, he frees his cock from his pants; it rolls up against his belly, and, *fuck,* it's long. And it's hard. A vein protrudes down the side of it. I wrap my hand around it, and Chase's hips jerk in response. I look up at him and he smiles at me, although it looks like he's in pain. "I like it when you touch me," he sighs.

I push my thumb up against the head of his cock and

watch a drip of precum spring onto the tip. Everyone's always told me the first time is scary and it hurts. But I just feel excited.

Chase puts his hands on my hips. "You're in charge, Jens."

I lift my hips and adjust his cock for me to sink down onto.

"Go as slow or as fast as you want..." Chase reassures me.

It takes a moment for me to fit him into me, but once he does, it feels right. I begin to lower myself onto him. My head dips back and a spasm of heat travels up my front.

Chase curses under his breath and I relish in the sound. I push my hips against him in a subtle, consistent rhythm. There's a bit of pain as he stretches me, but it's totally overshadowed by how full I feel, literally and metaphorically. This is exactly how I wanted my first time to feel. With someone I trust. With someone I can't resist.

Chase jerks his hips up into me and I gasp. "Sorry, sorry, I couldn't help it," he says, voice thick with want. "You feel so good."

"Do it again," I demand.

Chase grunts and heaves his hips up into me again. My nerves sparkle.

"Again."

He does so.

"Fuck me, Chase."

Again and again, he drives up into me, deeper with each stroke until he's pushing himself all the way to the hilt. My tits bounce with each pulse of his hips. I've never felt this good, so out of control.

"You're so beautiful," Chase groans. He runs a hand against my breasts. "So perfect."

I clasp his hand to my chest. He's striking upon nerves I didn't know existed from just touching myself. And they're so sensitive that my hips, thighs, legs, *everything* is shaking.

Chase slides his hands up my back and pulls me down onto his chest. He pushes his mouth up to my ear, continuing to drive up inside of me. "Fuck, you're tight," he growls.

All I can do is whimper. I'm a wreck.

"Can I go harder?"

I nod into his neck.

Chase locks his hands on my hips, holds me tight in place, and goes faster, harder. He grunts with every thrust of his hips. I hold onto the back of the couch for dear life, moaning his name again and again, louder and louder. Thank God my parents aren't home, or I'd be worried they could hear me all the way next door.

"Jenna..."

"Yes."

"Oh my god, Jenna," his voice is teetering higher in pitch. "I'm so close."

I cradle his head in my hand. "You're going to come, Chase?"

"Yes," he says, barely any voice in him.

If he comes, I'll come. There's no two ways about it. I'm being bathed in a glow of euphoria, so close to bursting.

"Come for me," I whisper in his ear. "Please, I need it."

"Not before you do," he says, shaking his head. "Not before you." Chase turns his head and captures my lips in his. Somehow, he pushes harder, harder, harder, and then –

I'm sent over the edge. A white heat rampages through me as the band of tension in my pelvis releases. It feels amazing. *He* feels amazing. I let out a tremendous gasp and feel myself contracting around his cock.

"Say my name," Chase rasps in my ear.

"Chase..."

He locks his forearms around my lower back, pulling us closer than I thought possible. "*Say my name!*" he roars.

"Chase, oh my god, come for me, please, Chase, please," I cry out.

And that pushes him right over the edge. I feel his warmth shoot deep inside me. Chase grunts loudly, stiltedly as if he doesn't have enough breath to keep it steady. My orgasm revisits me, echoing against his throbbing dick.

Finally, he lets out a sigh of surrender and his body goes limp under me.

We lay there, trying to catch our breath, for what feels like forever. Chase's hand starts to drift up and down my back. "You alright?"

I smile and lift my head. Our eyes lock on each other's. The darkness has faded from his irises, and I'm left with his sweet baby blues. "I'm great."

Chase smiles back. He takes one of my hands in his and kisses the back of it. I love the feeling of my hand in his. His hands are so big and capable. Strong. "Was that okay? For your first time?"

"Are you kidding?" I giggle. "That was a dream come true. Even with a broken leg."

"Fractured," he corrects as if they aren't the same.

"Fractured, sorry." After all he made me feel, I let it go, and w

e both laugh. Chase sighs heavily, his bare chest rising and falling. "What are we doing, Jenna? What are we..." He looks askance at the living room, as if all the baggage has just come into focus again.

"I don't know," I say. "But I can't pretend anymore that what's between you and me is just a friendship."

Chase smirks and pats my thigh. "Definitely not anymore..."

"Chase!" I smack his chest playfully.

He grins. "I'm sorry, I'm sorry. Couldn't resist."

I look down at the place where we still meet. He's gone soft inside me, but he's still there. I'm afraid of what it will feel like for him to leave.

Chase puts his hand against my cheek, tracing the curve of my skin. My eyes flutter shut. "I know what you mean, Jenna. We're not just friends," he says gently.

I lean closer to him. "Can we do this again?"

"I was hoping you'd say that," Chase grins.

"We'll just..." I run my hands up his arms, reveling in the feeling of his biceps. "We'll keep it a secret."

"Yes, of course," he says. "It'll be kind of fun. Sneaking around."

I giggle. "Yeah, yeah. Something only we know about."

"And never speak of again."

I swallow. That's the only right way to do it. After all, in a little over a month, he'll be able to walk around much easier without this cast, and I'll be going back to school soon after that. Our lives are completely different. We're too different for it to be anything more than a summer fling. "Perfect," I say confidently.

Chase smiles at me in a way that makes me feel like there's no one else in the world. And he kisses me again, chastely and dearly.

I don't want to admit it, and I certainly wouldn't out loud, but I wouldn't mind kissing Chase MacAllistair for the rest of my life. The rest of my fucking life.

9
___________

## CHASE

Jenna's in my thoughts long after she leaves in the afternoon. I don't even need to close my eyes to return to the image of her face when she came; slackened jaw, eyes rolling back, beautiful dark hair the messiest I've ever seen it.

Makes for a very awkward family dinner when I keep zoning out, remembering how Jenna moaned my name in my ear and how I came deep inside her as if I was claiming her.

"Chase!"

I snap my attention to Rachel and feel like God is about to smite me down. Her gray-blue eyes are looking at me like I've spilled coffee on her lap, almost furious. *Oh, fuck. What if Jenna told her? Already?!*

"Hello??? Pass the green beans!" she snaps at me.

"Rachel, be nice," Mom scolds her lightly.

"I've asked him like five times. He's in Lala land or something."

I pass the green beans and mumble an apology, although I'm not sure if it's for not passing the green beans or for much, much more than that. This guilt is going to eat me alive if I let it.

"Jenna and I are going to see a movie tonight," Rachel says, shuffling the beans onto her plate. "Can I borrow the car?"

"I'm taking the car tonight," Dan before taking a swig of his glass of milk.

Rachel's brow hardens, "Where are you going? You have training tomorrow at six."

"And I have training tonight at eight," he says, rolling his eyes.

"Oh my god," she groans. "I never thought I'd wish you had more of a social life."

"Why can't you take Jenna's car?" Dad asks.

She sighs, "Jenna's always driving, I feel bad. Plus, I owe her for all the time she's been spending with Chase."

I choke mid-bite.

"Easy, bro," Dan says and smacks my back. "Jesus, you good?"

"Dan, *language.*"

"He's choking!"

I grab my glass of water and knock it back. "I'm fine," I grunt, hitting my chest with my fist.

"What's the *matter* with you?" Rachel gapes at me.

"What's the matter with *you*?! Why are you being a total asshole?" Dan shoots back at her in my defense.

Dad holds his hands up. "Alright, kids, knock it off."

"No, she's always doing this," Dan says. "It's annoying."

"Doing what?" Rachel gripes.

"That thing you always do!"

Rachel and Dan start squabbling; I can't for the life of me figure out what the hell they're talking about. Something about that Twintuition, or whatever. I'm sure they've been bugging each other since they were in the womb. If anything, I'm glad the attention is off me. "Can I be done, mom?"

Mom looks at me with a resigned smile. "Chasey, you're thirty-five. Do what you want."

As if I needed the reminder that I'm sitting in my childhood home at thirty-five years old, stuck with my dumb fractured leg.

On top of fucking my sister's best friend.

<hr>

NEXT DAY, I'M NERVOUS. I CAN BARELY SIT STILL. So, I don't. I pace through the house as best I can, hobbling around on my crutches, trying to wear out my nasty nervous energy.

Jenna said she'd be over today. This was just before she kissed me goodbye and bashfully tucked a lock of her dark hair behind her ear. But as soon as the clock strikes noon, I'm convinced she's not going to show up.

I'm not usually like this. I can't be when I perform for crowds of thousands. Even with women I meet on tour, I'm not usually sweating it. Just move on to the next town, don't text back. It's not my most flattering look. But how can you blame me? Women throw themselves at musicians. And thank God they do. It's basically part of the musician's diet. The "sex" part of "sex, drugs, and rock'n'roll".

It was fun those first few years. Now it's just kind of hollow. After all, gone are the days of groupies. It would take a one-in-a-million woman who wants to go on the road and leave their life behind for you. And I've known forever that I would enjoy my life until I found my one and only. Because I've always wanted what Mom and Dad have. So why am I so amped up? Why does *she* make me feel like this?

Could it be...

"Hello?"

I come to at the sound of her voice. All other thoughts gone. I've been staring out the kitchen window lost in thought and didn't even hear her come in. "Hey!" I say, probably too excitedly, and round the corner back into the living room. As soon as I clap my eyes on Jenna, my mouth goes dry and I seem to forget every word I've ever known. I thought when I saw her again I'd be smooth and cool, even kiss her if I was getting the right vibe. That's not going to be possible when I stand stock still, gaping at her like I'm trying to catch flies.

Jenna's gorgeous. Has she done something different with her hair? Or is the green crop top she's wearing bringing out her eyes? The answer is both. *And*...now that I have her permission to look at her like she's a goddess, I see her as a goddess.

"You okay?" she asks in my silence.

"Uh...yeah. I'm okay. Great. I'm great," I stutter. "It's good to see you."

Jenna smiles shyly. "You too."

Both of us stand there for a moment like we're video game characters but the person playing the game has walked away. Idling. Wondering what comes next.

Jenna holds up the bag in her hands which I hadn't noticed at first. "I brought tacos."

"Oh. Yum," I say.

Jenna doesn't reply, just smiles sweetly and breezes past me. It's true, I could eat. But I've got other things on my mind, what with her short shorts showing so much of her thighs. I watch her at the kitchen counter unpacking the tacos that are wrapped up in tin foil. "Have you ever had tacos from that place in the strip mall with the weird striped awning?" she asks, not looking up from unpacking the bag.

"No, I don't think so," I say. My eyes drift down her back to her bare waist; there's a small dip in her back. It'd be a perfect place to rest my hand. Would be easy to slide my hand into her waistband and grab a handful of her –

"How's your spice tolerance?"

Jenna turns around with little plastic containers of salsa. I chuckle. "It's fine. Good even."

She narrows her eyes at me. "I somehow don't believe you." Then, she turns back to organizing the food.

Fuck, I can't do this. I can't just pretend I'm not totally desperate for her. I make my way over to her quietly.

"They have this amazing horchata that I just – "

I touch her waist. Jenna lifts her chin to look up at me, like a doe who's been spotted in a forest. I can't resist her plush, parted lips. I kiss her firmly, pull her up close to me, feel her hands find purchase on my chest. When the kiss breaks, I whisper, "Hi."

"Hi," she whispers back, eyelids low.

I drift my fingers up and down her lower back. "It's good to see you."

Jenna giggles, blushing. She wraps her arms around my waist and props her chin up on my chest looking up at me. I wish I could embrace her the way I want, but the damn crutches make it hard to get my grip on her. "Is this weird?" she asks quietly.

I push a lock of her dark hair away from her forehead. "No. Do you feel weird?"

She bites her lip in thought. "A little. But that's not a bad thing," she clarifies.

"Oh good. As long as it's a good weird."

"Yes, a very good weird," Jenna says sweetly. She rises on her tiptoes and gives me a small kiss. "You hungry?"

"Yeah, yeah, I could eat..." I reply, although not in the way she's thinking. I kiss her again on her lips and she melts into my arms easily. The food can wait. I have to have her. "I want to taste you."

Jenna doesn't respond right away; her breath changes the slightest bit.

"Because I bet you taste fucking amazing," I say, unable to keep myself from smiling at the thought.

Her fingers curl around my biceps. "Chase, the food's going to get cold."

"I don't care about that," I mutter, trailing a line of kisses down from her ear to her neck.

"The ice will melt..."

I plant a wet kiss on her jugular. "So what?"

She whimpers slightly at the feeling of my teeth pulling on the skin of her neck. "Chase..."

"Can I?" I ask, gently guiding her up against the kitchen island.

I hear her swallow. "No one's ever...I've never..."

I hook my hands under her arms and lift her in a fluid motion onto the counter. She gasps into my mouth as I kiss her forcefully again. I run my hands up her bare thighs to her hips, letting my fingers sink into the curve of her waist. "I'll be gentle, Jenna. I'll be so gentle."

Jenna draws her head back to look at me. Though there's some trepidation in her face, her pupils are wide enough to swallow me whole. She shakes her head the littlest bit. "You don't have to be gentle, Chase."

I plant my hands on either side of her. Jenna places her hands on my cheeks, scraping her fingers up from my beard to my hair. A chill runs down my spine from her touch. I smile at her. "I just want to make you feel good."

Jenna smiles back. Her knees tighten around my sides, drawing me into her. I can feel the heat coming off of her pussy; it makes me so hard. But this isn't about me. I can wait. She kisses me softly, permitting me to go further.

"Take off your shorts, baby," I instruct her.

While she does that, I reach for one of the stools on the island, one of the two where Rachel and Dan almost always eat their breakfast. I yank it so it's right in front of her and I sit down, right between her legs. I wouldn't normally find a comfortable seat for matters such as these. In fact, it's hard to consider I need a little bit of help when I just want to devour her completely. But my fucking leg makes it difficult for absolutely everything and certainly ruins the spontaneity of something like this.

Jenna repositions herself in front of me, leaning on her hands, showing off her cute little panties. White and lacy, with a little bow right at the top. "Thought you might want to do this part yourself," she says coyly, wiggling her hips to the edge of the counter.

"How did you know?" I reply. I lean into her and press a line of kisses from her belly button to her pelvis, planting the last kiss to her pussy through her underwear. Jenna sighs at the feeling. I inhale the pungent, sensual aroma of her pussy deeply. I can't get enough. "You smell so good," I mumble in between her legs.

Jenna runs her hand through my hair and I look up at her, our eyes meeting. She chews on the inside of her lower lip nervously, but I can tell she's excited by the way the corners of her lips perk up at the sides.

"You're so beautiful, Jenna," I murmur and then kiss the insides of her thighs. "So perfect..."

"Not perfect," she says.

"No, no..." I hook my fingers through the delicate fabric of her panties and pull them down just enough to reveal her lower lips. They look delicious. "Totally perfect," I repeat before pressing my mouth to her pussy and delving my tongue inside.

Jenna's thighs tighten around me and she curses. I'm in heaven, lapping her up. She tastes amazing. Sweet and tangy and like every good thing. I nudge her red, pulsing clitoris with my nose. Jenna jumps beneath me and I grip her thighs so she can't move out of my grasp.

"Oh my god, Chase..."

Her utterance of my name makes me lightheaded. I press my lips tighter to her, working faster and harder. I encircle her clitoris with my tongue. Jenna clutches my head from behind, her fingernails on my scalp. I hum in pleasure; it reverberates down her thighs and I just know it's driving her crazy. Her breath is growing shallower and more strained.

I flip my eyes up to her, catching her pretty hazel eyes with mine. Her mouth hangs open in euphoric bliss. No man's ever made her feel like this. I don't want to fuck this up. I pop her clitoris between my lips and begin to suck. Jenna keens loudly and links her ankles around my back.

God, I wish I could watch this back. Wish I could have the image of her head tilting back and her mouth falling open forever. I could use a sample of her moans on a track in the studio. That'd be something else.

I can feel her getting close. Her hips are jerking, trying to fuck my face, and her stomach muscles are shaking uncontrollably. I come up for a breath. "Let go, Jenna. Come on my face."

Jenna weakly nods, and I return to my pattern of tongue

flicking and clit sucking until she whines loudly. She takes my head in both her hands and bends forward over me. Her pussy pulses in my mouth, walls teasing and clenching my tongue. I try to lick her clit once more, but she bristles. It's too sensitive. I won't push her. Not today. Not her first time. I run my hands up to her waist. Her essence covers my mouth and my beard. I lick my lips. Still tastes like heaven.

Jenna's stomach heaves with effort as she tries to catch her breath. "Oh my god, Chase...you're really good at that."

"I've had a lot of practice," I say and immediately regret it. I don't want her to think I'm just some manwhore using her up. "I mean..."

Jenna laughs before I can amend. "Oh, shut up. We get it, you're famous."

I'm glad she's so good-humored about it. "Did it feel good?" I ask hopefully.

Jenna nods and then runs her thumb over my lip and through my beard. "I'm all over your face."

"That's the way I like it," I reply. "Save it for later."

"Ew, gross," she cackles.

We stare at one another for a few moments, taking in this moment. I've just had her for lunch on the kitchen island, adding insult to injury to my family and this secret we're keeping. I can't help but be turned on by it, though. Jenna's been the only thing keeping me sane this past month through my recovery. I need a little fun. I need to be a little bad.

"Is it weird to be starving after coming?" Jenna says sheepishly.

I laugh and kiss her stomach, squeezing her thighs. "Not at all. Come on. You were working hard."

She thwaps me on the shoulder playfully.

We have a delicious meal of room-temperature tacos

and watered-down horchata on the deck, but I couldn't care less about the food. All I'm focused on is Jenna and the way she watches and looks around nervously, like she's afraid that if someone saw us, they'd be able to tell that she was just having her pussy eaten.

"You're acting like a meerkat," I say eventually.

Her eyes snap to me. "What are you talking about?"

"You're looking around like –" I mimic what she was doing, although my impression skews more meerkat than human.

Jenna laughs and finally relaxes a bit. "I don't look like that!"

"Uh, yeah, you do. Just chill out," I say before polishing off an al pastor taco. "Nobody's looking."

She takes a sip of horchata. "I felt like I was wearing a scarlet letter at dinner last night."

I chuckle. "You think your parents could smell the sex on you?"

"Chase!"

"Sorry, I'm just – "

"It freaked me out a little," she says, leaning on her hand. "I don't know. They never pry too much. But I just kept thinking that one of them was eventually going to notice something different about me."

I consider what she's said. "Do you think there's something different about you?"

Jenna's brow furrows. "Yeah...yeah, I guess I do." Her eyes find mine. "I feel like I'm free now."

I try to smile casually, but my heart is singing. That's a big fucking compliment. I'm honored to have been a part of that for her. Proud, even. Maybe once she goes back to school, she'll have the best semester of her life and be a maneater. That thought gives me a sad sinking feeling inside. *Be here now, Chase.*

The rest of the afternoon, we waste away lazily on the couch. However, instead of sitting at opposite ends, we're intertwined. I rest my head on her lap and she plays with my hair while we listen to some music. She picked a folk playlist with the likes of Bob Dylan, Townes Van Zandt, and Joni Mitchell. I can't help but be taken with it. As a musician, how can you not be inspired by people like that?

"I wish I could write songs like Bob Dylan," I murmur.

Jenna traces the shell of my ear with her finger. "I bet you could."

I shrug. "I can't write lyrics."

"Chase..."

"Or, let me be clearer, I *don't* write lyrics," I say with a sigh. "Nobody thinks that a drummer might have something to say."

Jenna's fingers follow the curve of my jaw. I close my eyes. "You should just start writing. I'm sure your band-mates would love what you come up with."

"Naw, it'd all be lovesick poetry," I chuckle. "No one wants that."

"I do."

"Yeah, but you think I'm cute, so – "

"Woah, woah, woah!" she cuts in. "Who said I think you're cute?!"

I look up at her with a grin. "Well, I guess I think you think I'm cute."

"Mm...fair," she concedes. "You should write something, Chase. If that's what you want to do."

I huff. "If only it were that easy."

"Yeah, I get it."

We sit in silence a little longer. I tighten my hand on her thigh. "You'll get a job, Jenna. I know you will."

"I..." she hesitates. "Thank you. But that honestly hasn't been much on my mind lately."

I wonder what *has* been on her mind. Me, probably. Not to be self-centered, but that just seems true at this point. My head is on her lap, for Christ's sake.

"You know, I've spent so much time at home with my parents and..." she speaks delicately and measuredly, as if afraid to share what she's really feeling. "I don't know, it's silly."

"You can tell me," I say, raising my head to look at her.

Jenna smiles at me endearingly. "Okay, well, don't read into it."

"I won't." I think sometimes she forgets that because I'm older than her, I'm not like boys her age. I've lived more life. I don't scare as easily. And Jenna could never scare me away. Unlike boys, I know what I want. I've always known. It has just been a waiting game for me.

"My parents are really good together. I've always thought that," she says quietly. "But this is the longest I've really spent at home with them now that I'm in college. Usually, I'm running around doing internships or working a shitty restaurant job. But this summer, I've been forced to take it slow, you know? And so, I see them a lot more and they're just..." I hear a razor's edge of sentiment in her voice. "They love each other so much. And they love me so much."

"Of course, they do," I say.

"And like, I want that. For me. In the future. And it's so scary because finding someone you love and creating a family...so much of that is out of my control. So much of that is, like, chance and timing and how fucking scary is that?"

I sit up a bit to get a look at her face. Jenna's eyes are swimming with tears she probably didn't mean to have. "Come here, sweetheart," I murmur and pull her into my chest. This girl is fourteen years younger than me, but it hits me that we are exactly the same. We want the same thing out of life. And I can't help to wonder, what if...

Jenna rests her head there, nestles into me and clings to me. I wrap my arms around her. "You'll be okay. It'll happen." I almost scoff at myself. "You're so young, you've got so much time."

I have to bite my tongue as I console her. Because deep down I know that if she asked, I'd give her everything she wanted. Every. Single. Thing.

10

———

JENNA

"I'm surprised you agreed to hang out today," Rachel says, flipping through dresses on the clearance rack quickly.

I look at her quizzically. "Surprised?"

"Yeah!" Rachel pipes up and pulls out a long purple dress with little blue flowers. "What do you think?"

I make a face of disgust and she rolls her eyes. "You know I'm not into florals."

"But florals are in, Jens," she argues and then goes right back to looking.

I watch her for a moment and then ask again, "Why were you surprised?"

"You've said you're busy the past few times I've asked to hang out."

I raise my eyebrows. That can't be true, can it?

"If I didn't know better, I'd say you have a secret boyfriend you're hiding from me," she teases with a knowing look in her blue eyes.

It takes everything in me not to look guilty. The truth is that every time I'm around Rachel now, I feel guilty. It's been two weeks since Chase and I slept together for the first time. And ever since then we've been fooling around pretty much every weekday. It's been perfect. Because nothing has changed between us. We still give each other shit and laugh a lot. We play games and watch movies and talk. And now we have sex too.

And, boy, do I love the sex.

Of course, it's all fun and games when we're together. But when we're not...I feel so guilty. When Rachel or Dan text me and I see their names on my phone, I get this deep sense of dread. How am I supposed to look them in the eyes when I'm fooling around with their older brother behind their backs? I guess, you could say we are now friends with benefits.

Okay, maybe a little more than friends...but certainly a lot of benefits.

I guess now that she mentioned it, I have been going out of my way to be busier. I've started spending more time with my parents and I've taken up a new exercise routine that has me in the gym longer. I don't have good excuses for not hanging out with her. They're just excuses. And I've needed them.

"I'm sorry, Rach, I've been – "

"Busy," she cuts me off dryly. "I know." She pulls a raspberry skirt off the rack and holds it up.

I make a not-bad-not-good face, lips curling down, shoulders shrugging.

"You're no help," she says, hanging the skirt back on the rack.

"I'm sorry, this stuff just isn't my style," I say. "You would look great in it." Rachel's style is louder than mine. She walks across campus in her high heels and brightly colored blazers like she's walking a catwalk. Meanwhile, I prefer to be a bit more understated.

Rachel drops the skirt back on the rack and walks past me. "Come on, let's go somewhere else."

She leads me through the mall to the Victoria's Secret, saying she needs to get some no-show thongs for tighter dresses. I follow her without much of a thought and browse the store with her until she brings the subject of my absence up again. "I'm just getting jealous," she says as she sorts through a stack of underwear, looking for her size.

"Jealous?" I ask.

"Yeah! I mean, Chase sees you like almost every day. That's totally unfair," she grumbles and moves on to the next display.

I feel my heart thudding in my mouth. If she was actually suspicious something was going on, Rachel wouldn't be coy about it. She'd ask me point blank. But her invoking Chase's name in this conversation is certainly unsettling.

"Like, you're *my* best friend. And I barely see you."

"Rach, I see you all the time."

"But not as much as you used to!" she says back. She's smiling. Rachel always smiles, even when she's hurting. "I'm just saying, I miss you. Don't let Chase take up all of your allotted MacAllistair time."

I sigh. She's right. I'm letting Chase get in the way of our friendship. It's why I tried to resist him in the first place. It won't last forever, though. Once his leg is better, he won't be next door every day, and he'll be onto the next big thing in his career. And I'll be back at school. This is just for now. "I'm sorry, Rach. I didn't even realize."

Her smile turns from edgy to grateful. "It's okay. Just...I miss you. I want to see you more than I do."

Growing up next door to your best friend is one of the

greatest gifts in the world. I'm only three months older than Rachel and Dan. We've basically been friends since her birth. We have a special bond because of it. But that also means that my absence is more noticeable than it would be if we lived on different streets or in different neighborhoods. I'll need to be more careful. "How can I make it up to you?"

"Stop acting like I'm dragging you around to stores like I'm your mother and actually have some fun, maybe?" Rachel says, jamming a finger into my ribs.

I squeal at the tickling sensation on my side. "Rach!"

"I'm going to go look at the clearance," she says with a grin and walks off toward the back of the store.

The only times I've been in Victoria's Secret were to buy sports bras or Love Spell when I was obsessed with smelling like peaches in middle school. I don't usually piddle about looking at the lingerie and underwear. I meander around the store for a bit, turning my nose up at the strappy, needlessly complicated lingerie sets. It all seems too extra and unnecessary.

That is, until I come upon a set highlighted under a spotlight in one of the displays. It's a matching bra and thong, electric blue, with thick straps and mesh all brought together with silver hardware in the middle. It's...hardcore, honestly. And sexy. I don't know if I could pull something like that off, but...

Maybe I could try.

---

"THAT'S A CUTE LITTLE DRESS," CHASE COMPLIMENTS as I return to the deck with two glasses of lemonade.

I look down at the little dark green shift dress I've donned. Not my usual look, but I've got to keep the secret of what's underneath. "Oh, you like it?"

"Yeah, it makes you look like a mom in the nineties. Which, believe it or not, I think is a compliment," he clarifies, tilting back his head. "It's very sexy."

I blush, "*Chase.*"

"Sorry, do you think the birds overheard me? Do you think they're going to tell on me?" Chase grins.

I set the glasses out on the table, but I don't sit. I'm a little restless. I've never done anything like this before. "I'm just not used to being called sexy."

"That's insane," he says boisterously. "I hope you know how absolutely ridiculous that is. You're like..."

"Sexy?" I interject with a hand on my hip.

"You said it, not me," he says and then takes a sip of the lemonade. He sighs happily and looks out at the trees.

I've been waiting all day for my big reveal. And, of course, I can't show him what's underneath my dress right here on the deck out in the open, but I can definitely tease him. "Want to play a game?"

Chase looks at me with a suspicious smile. "What kind of game?"

"You're asking me that like I'm going to get you in trouble."

"Wouldn't be the first time," he says with a waggle of his eyebrows.

I laugh and trace my sandalled foot against the wooden floor. "Okay, well it's a little bit of trouble."

"I knew it! And I'm ready. I won't be hustled by you again, Jenna," Chase says eagerly.

"It's not blackjack," I say rolling my eyes. "It's a guessing game."

"Oh. Twenty questions? I am good at that game. We

play that when we tour on the bus. Great for when you can't sleep."

I shake my head and wander over to the deck railing, leaning up against it. "Not twenty questions."

"Okay, what is it? Tell me," he replies. Chase is so cute when he's excited. He wears this evergreen smile and his blue eyes twinkle like the clearest lake you could find.

"I just thought you could maybe guess what color my panties are."

That evergreen smile fades. I've taken him off-guard which was my goal. "Your panties?"

"And my bra," I add. "Because they match. And I think you'd like them. But...I'll only show them to you if you can guess what color they are."

The smile returns. "That's a game I can't say I've ever played."

"Does it sound like fun?"

"Hell, yeah. Obviously," Chase nods. I'm sure if he could, he'd leap up and try and see them himself.

"And to make things *interesting*," I say, lolling my head to the side. "For every time you guess incorrectly, *you* have to take off a piece of clothing.

Chase scoffs and then realizes I'm not joking. "I'm wearing like three pieces of clothing."

"So, you better get it right," I say with a smug smirk.

It's a standoff between Chase and me, waiting for the other to give in. I'm not budging and he knows it. "Do I get to see them even if I don't guess the color?"

"I'll consider it."

"You're cruel, Jenna," he groans.

"I'm not cruel. I'm fair," I say. I love this power I have over him. He wants me so badly. "First guess?"

Chase eyes me for a moment and then says, "Do a little walk for me."

"A walk?"

"Yeah, like you're a model. Show me what you got."

I roll my eyes. "I don't have a model walk, but *okay*..." I traverse the deck, swinging my hips and tossing my hair, giving my best Gigi Hadid. Chase hoots and hollers like he's my biggest fan. "There."

"And give me a twirl, please."

"How is this going to help you guess the color of my underwear?"

"I have my ways, now –" Chase holds up a finger and gestures it in a circle. "Twirl, my dear."

I twirl around half-heartedly, my dress splaying out around my knees. "Okay. Your guess."

"Hmmm...well. I feel like you're a classic kind of girl. Not playing it safe but sticking with what works. But then again, you could be tricking me and have gone for something totally off the wall," Chase thinks out loud. His eyes are zeroed in on me as if I'm a specimen in a lab. Makes it even funnier when the thing he's having to figure out is the color of my lingerie. "Black."

I pout my lips and shake my head. "Strip."

"Dammit. Played it safe. I knew I shouldn't have," he grumbles. "Okay. Shirt's coming off."

As soon as Chase lifts his shirt over his head, my heart speeds up. "Maybe we should go inside if – "

"Oh, who cares? It's hot. It's Texas. People won't bat an eye if my shirt is off," he says and tosses the t-shirt to the side. He relaxes back into his chair, showing off his broad chest. I salivate at the trail of hair that goes down from his belly button to his pants. "You, on the other hand..."

I know my face is red and I desperately wish I was better at controlling that. "Okay, second guess."

Chase inclines his head back. "Purple."

I give him a thumbs down and blow a raspberry.

"Fuck! I thought – "

"You think purple is 'off the wall'?" I say incredulously.

"Well, I don't know! Listen, not a lot of girls plan their underwear for me. I've never done this before," he says, running a hand back through his beautiful blond locks in frustration.

Chase pulls at the waistband of his shorts. He's stuck wearing athletic shorts and sweatpants with the cast. Most other things won't go over them. "Help me, would you?"

I go over and help guide the shorts off his legs. I have to scold him for trying to look down my dress to peep the color of my bra. As I help Chase, we are both quiet. I can already see he's semi-hard in his boxer briefs. "Maybe *now* we should go inside?" I ask.

He shrugs. "No one can see us back here. Come on, Jens. Live a little."

Chase now sits clad only in his underwear while I stand across from him in my little dress. He's a sight for sore eyes. I love the whorls of hair that run up his long legs. He's entirely a man and that makes me feel entirely like a woman. "Last guess, baby."

Chase rests his chin in his hand, scratching his beard in contemplation. "Not black, not purple...you're not a pink girl. Red is too basic. It's not –" Suddenly, he snaps and points at me. "*Trick question.* You're not wearing anything at all."

My eyes bug out at him and I burst into a ream of laughter. "You really think *I wouldn't wear underwear?!*"

"No, come on. I'm right. I know I'm right."

"I'm wearing underwear, Chase. I promise you that."

"Then prove it! Show me!"

"Not before you take off your briefs!" I announce gleefully, pointing to his crotch.

Chase huffs.

"You can't take off your underwear out here!" I say in a loud whisper.

"It's my house," he says smugly. "So, what if someone sees?"

"Chase! They won't just see your dick; they'll see *me* looking at your dick!"

Chase thumbs the band of his underwear and looks at me. "We can go inside if you want, but I don't think anyone can see us back here, Jenna." He traces his thumb back and forth under the elastic. "Why not be a little dangerous?"

I've gone from losing my virginity to being deviant in the span of just a couple of weeks. I guess that's what finding a guy you're obsessed with can do to you. But this seems...okay, it seems absolutely unhinged and yet...

Fuck, I'm horny.

"Fine," I say, trying to show I'm disdainful but not doing a good job of it.

Chase pushes his underwear down, releasing his cock from the tight constraints. He's still not fully hard, but he's already large and thick. He's able to free his good leg but lets the underwear hang around his other thigh. "There. No more clothes."

"No more clothes," I repeat and give him a sly smile.

"Can I see now?"

A breeze passes over us, cutting the Texas heat with coolness. I can't believe we're really doing this outside.

"No one's going to see, baby. I promise."

I believe him. I *trust* him. The trust has been implicit

since I've met him which is why this spiraled out of control the way it did. I mean, he's a MacAllistair. And the MacAllistair family is almost like my second family.

Almost.

I walk over to him and stand in front of him, taking my skirt up in my hands. I pull it up incrementally, relishing in his anticipation. "Are you ready, Chase?"

"Been ready," he says, licking his lips.

I pull the dress up to my waist and reveal to him the electric blue panties I bought just a couple of days earlier.

"Blue? You've got to be kidding me..."

"Wouldn't have guessed it, hm?"

"Not at all, ever," Chase says. He grabs my thighs and pulls me in between his legs. "Blue...fuck, these look great on you." He strokes my legs up and down and then grabs my ass in both his hands. "Jesus Christ, what do I do with you?"

I giggle and run my hands through his hair. "Anything you want."

"Yeah?" He presses a line of kisses up my belly. "Anything?"

I swallow. Anything is a big word, especially for a guy who has done most sexual acts under the sun and a girl who lost her virginity less than a month ago. But with him, I feel like I can be free. I really do trust him. "Yeah. Anything," I say softly.

Chase smiles up at me. He's not going to abuse that privilege. He knows what I'm worth and won't hesitate to show me. "Take off your dress."

I follow his instruction, revealing the matching electric blue bra with the mesh and the straps. He inhales sharply. "Fucking gorgeous, Jenna. Wow."

"Got it for you."

"What did I do to deserve that?" Chase asks with a wonky smile.

I shrug. So many things I could think of off the top of my head.

Chase's fingers curl into the panties and he yanks them down over my thighs. My breath sticks in my throat. "Chase..."

"I want to have you right here."

I look over my shoulder at the empty yard. The deck is mostly veiled. You can't see my house unless you're at the very front of it. And the trees are dense beyond the fence line.

Chase kisses the knot of my pubic bone. "Can I?"

I nod. "Yeah. Yes."

He jerks me around and pulls me down onto his lap, right onto his rigid cock. I gasp at the quick feeling of fullness. I've gotten used to how big he is and how he stretches me, but the shock gets me every time. "Ride me, baby," he growls into my ear.

I begin to bob my hips on his, sliding up and down the length of his cock. Chase curses under his breath from time to time, his hands curving around my hips and ass. His grip is tight, almost painful, but I don't mind. Adds to the feeling that he wants me.

"I wish I could..." he begins but stops as a wave of arousal hits him.

"Wish you could..." I echo and take one of his hands in mine. I hold onto it tightly as my nerves set alight and press it up against my ribs.

"I wish I could really have you...the way I want..." he grunts.

I roll my head to the side as he strikes a deep, sensitive point inside me. "How's that?"

Suddenly, mustering an enormous amount of strength, Chase pushes himself up from the deck chair, still inside me. I lean forward and catch myself on the matching ottoman with a huff of shock. He thrusts deep inside me, almost throwing me off balance. I pull one knee up onto the ottoman to balance myself, gripping the cushion for balance.

I don't know how he's doing it, driving inside me while balancing on one leg, but he's strong and adept. I reach back and touch the top of his cast. "Chase, your leg," I manage despite the pleasure building inside me.

"I got it," he says forcefully. I don't question it any further. If he wants me like this, he'll have me like this. I love how he takes what he wants. I love that he wants me.

It takes everything in me not to moan. I'm already self-conscious about it when we fuck inside, where no one can hear us. But outside? Even if no one can see us, someone would hear us. I bite down on my lip to keep quiet, only releasing small whimpers from deep in my throat.

Chase slides one of his wide hands under the fabric of my bra. He massages my breast tenderly, a contrast to the roughness with which he's driving in and out of me. His thumb and forefinger squeeze my nipple, sending a shower of sparks down my front. I jerk hard against him.

"You like that?"

I nod heavily with a mewl.

"Shhh...shhh..." Chase caresses the fold of my waist and hip. "I know you feel good, baby, but you have to be quiet."

His hand moves down from my chest to the place where we meet, his cock sliding in and out of me with repetitive slick sounds. He pushes the button of my clitoris, filling my whole body with tickling warmth. Chase rubs it in circles, continuing to push inside me without respite. I can't take it much longer. The muscles in my stomach are seizing and jumping. I know it's coming.

"I'm so close, I'm so close," I mutter as quietly as I can. "Holy shit."

"Good girl," Chase coos. "Come for me."

Just a few more slick pulses inside me and my entire body shudders. An electric current zips up my front harshly, lightning and thunder at once. I bend forward and bury my face in the ottoman cushion so I can scream. My core tightens around Chase's hardness, inviting him to come with me and, with just a couple more pulses, he does.

Chase curses under his breath as his hips stutter with orgasm. The heat of his seed drives me mad, feels so good to know I caused that.

In the afterglow of our pleasure, reality settles over us. Outside. On the deck. On top of all the things that already weigh heavily on my brain after Chase and I became intimate. Once Chase releases me, I immediately rush to put on my dress again. I don't even care I'm not cleaned up underneath it. But if someone saw..."You're a bad influence, Chase," I say playfully, although a part of me sort of believes it.

"Me? You're the one parading around talking about your underwear," he ribs back.

I turn back to him. His shirt is still off, but he's managed his briefs back on and is now trying to get into a good position to pull his gym shorts over his cast. "You're going to hurt yourself like that," I say quietly.

"I've got it."

I let him struggle just another moment before I go over to Chase and kneel before him. "I took them off, I should help put them back on."

Chase looks at me, trying to discern whether he really

needs to ask for help or not. I take the gym shorts and pull them slowly up over his legs, making sure the elastic band doesn't snap against his skin. When things are in the name of sex and fun, Chase doesn't mind asking for what he needs. But when he's reminded of his situation, that becomes harder. I kiss him gently below his belly button. It's a spot I've come to really love over the past two weeks, the spot that leads to something that feels darker and dangerous, but also so vulnerable and soft.

Chase cups the back of my head in his hand, gingerly scratching his fingers through my hair. "Come sit with me."

We sit on the deck chair, me curled up on his lap, balanced on his good leg. I trace my fingers up and down the expanse of his chest. We exchange small kisses from time to time, bantering from time to time about meaningless, unmemorable things.

"You're so fun, Jenna," Chase mutters after a while. "I have so much fun with you."

My stomach twists. For some reason, that doesn't feel like a compliment. It reminds me that this is temporary. The fun can't last forever. And the expiration is fast approaching, with school starting mid-August and Chase going back to his fast-paced, big life when he is fully recovered. I know it will be some time still, but I know the stakes. Because I'm just a girl. With electric blue panties, but still. Just a girl.

I wrap my arms around him and bury my face in his neck.

"So sweet…" Chase says, rubbing his hand up and down my back and kissing the crown of my head.

I don't think he realizes that there are tears in my eyes and I'm biting the inside of my cheek to keep from crying.

## 11

## CHASE

"I think another week and then we can take this cast off," the doctor drones as he looks at my new x-rays. "We'll get you set up with a physical therapist to get your leg back to proper use. And then you'll be good as new."

What a relief. One more week with this godforsaken wall of plaster on my leg. I'll be able to walk again, play drums the way I want again, and I'll be able to...move back into my apartment.

I don't want to think about leaving my parents' house. It's been so nice. All the quality time with them and getting to know Rachel and Dan better now that they're grown up.

And Jenna.

Jenna's the sorest spot in my getting better. Because as soon as I leave, that's it. Right? I mean, we haven't spoken about what an ending will look like between us. It just seems implicit. Like how I move on to the next town when I'm on tour. There's nothing to be sentimental about. That's just life.

I'll go back to my apartment, get ready to record the next album. Jenna will go back to school, be consumed with classes, and trying to find that elusive internship or job. We'll go our separate ways. Maybe see each other in passing at Christmas or Thanksgiving. And we won't ever speak of what's been happening between us, but we'll always know.

Why is that thought so painful?

Jay brought me here but he had to leave right after. Said he had an appointment he just couldn't miss. *I wonder if it has anything to do with a woman?* Lucas picks me up and drives me back home. I haven't seen him since the tour ended and he's in really good spirits.

"I've already come up with a few song concepts. I can't wait to get into the studio," he says excitedly as we breeze down the highway.

I shift slightly in my seat. "That's awesome, man."

"Yeah. I mean, it'll be hard to top the last album, but this one has to *fuck*," Lucas adds. "It has to go *hard*."

"Yeah, it does have to fuck."

"Maybe you can take a look at some of the lyrics I've already written out. You always give good feedback," he says with a casual shrug.

Lucas and Dylan normally write most of our lyrics. And they're really good. Poetic, but direct. Searing and sentimental. The perfect amount of light and shade. "Totally, man. Listen –" I get a burst of courage, "I'd love to get some more acoustic stuff on the album."

He considers, narrowing his eyes on the road. As the vocalist, Lucas definitely has had his moments of being a diva and has vetoed ideas in the past. "What were you thinking?"

"I don't know, just really get down to our roots. A little folk, a little country. Make it ours, of course, but let's really show our inner Texan, you feel me?" I say. "I already have a few ideas for lyrics and – "

"You're writing lyrics? Right on, man," Lucas says with a lopsided smile. "Finally. We've all been waiting for you to write something."

I scoff, "Really?"

"Yeah! You're always the one who can fill in my blanks. It was only a matter of time before you pulled your weight and wrote one yourself," he replies with a wink.

I'm speechless. I didn't want to step on his toes by suggesting it, but hearing that the whole band is behind me is all I needed to get me writing again. When I get back home, I immediately start fleshing out my ideas in an old spiral notebook.

Jenna's been gone three days, visiting one of her friends in Waco. And it's been pretty lonely most days. But now that my mind is running a mile a minute with ideas, I'm totally engrossed. I'll have to thank her. I probably wouldn't have had the courage to mention it to Lucas if not for our conversations about it. And I probably wouldn't have all the ideas I'm having too.

They're all about her, or some form of her. They're about forbidden love, about youth, about someone unexpected.

As cliché as it is, Jenna is my muse.

Later in the afternoon, I get a text from Jenna.

*Hope you're keeping busy ;)*

We hadn't had each other's numbers until she went on this trip. We figured it would be harmless to text here and there, just keep in touch. And it's been nice to still be able to talk to her, although I've had to put her in my phone under a different name because I'm paranoid Rachel will see she's texting me and ask about it.

Even though I'm a grown man, it's hard not to read into text messages. A winky face? What does that mean?

I reply.

*Doing my best. Wish I could keep busy other ways...*

I send that and then add a winky face in a separate message. Just a bit later, she responds.

*You're so naughty.*

My cock jumps in my pants. She texts again.

*Getting on the road now. See you soon.*

Not soon enough. Time goes by sluggishly. It's a fairly normal evening. Normal Wednesday night dinner. Normal conversation over the dinner table. Normal Mom-and-Dad-watch-their-show-while-Chase-third-wheels night. But my anticipation is mounting.

It's late when I see headlights in the window and hear her car pulling into the driveway next door.

*Welcome home.*

She doesn't get back to me for a while, but when she does, my heart melts.

*Wish I could see you right now.*

If I were in better shape, it'd be no problem. I could sneak out and we could hop in the car, drive somewhere, even go do something. See a movie, get dinner...

Now I just sound like a sap. That would be a date and what Jenna and I are doing is *not* dating.

I think I'd like it to be, though. Before I can reply, my phone starts ringing. I answer it without thinking. "Hello?"

"Hi, Chase."

Her voice is just as sweet over the phone as it is in person. Even sweeter since I haven't heard her talk in a few days. I look around. I'm alone in the living room. Mom and Dad have already settled into bed. Dan knocked out extra early from a rough practice. And Rachel is upstairs doing some studying for an exam. "Hey, you," I answer quietly.

"It's good to hear your voice."

I smile to myself.

"I'm at my bedroom window. Can you see me?"

I frown bewilderedly and limp over to the living room window. I can see the corner of her window from here, but I can't see inside.

"Get somewhere where you can see me."

"Okay, give me a minute." She doesn't have to tell me twice. I know exactly where I can see her from. I go through the kitchen to the back deck, out to the yard. That'll give me the best view.

"I see you," she says in a sing-song voice.

And I see her, right through her bedroom window with the purple curtains. There's a lamp on, casting an orange glow through the room. I can't make out all the glorious details of her, but I can see her motions. She waves.

"There you are..."

Jenna sighs contentedly. "I missed you."

My heart flutters. "I missed you, too."

"You look so pretty there in the dark," she giggles.

I blush and scratch the back of my head. "Pretty, huh?"

"Yeah, you're so pretty," she replies. "I'm going to get ready for bed. You want to watch?"

My jaw drops. "Um, yeah. Yes. Definitely. Absolutely."

Jenna giggles over the phone. I hear the rustling of fabric and I see her lift her shirt over her head, immediately exposing her chest.

"*Jenna*," I whisper.

"Wish you could touch me right now," she says.

"Me too. God..." I can barely believe she was a virgin. She knows how to tease me so well.

Jenna runs her hands over her exposed flesh, around the buxomness of her breasts, the soft curve of her belly. She turns away from the window and pulls the mane of her dark chocolatey curls into a messy bun. The soft plane of her back looks like a perfect place to kiss and nestle my face against. I can imagine her smell from here, her sweet, tangerine perfume mixed with her pheromones. Ever since I've had her, smelled her, tasted her, her musk is impossible to ignore. I wish she was right here with me so I could –

"Chase, what are you doing?"

I reflexively hang up the call and throw my phone, letting out a yelp of surprise, finding Rachel behind me in her sleep clothes and her reading glasses. Her arms are crossed over her chest. "You scared the shit out of me," I grumble.

"You left the door open," she says, jerking her thumb back toward the sliding glass doors that lead from the kitchen to the deck. "You're going to let the mosquitoes in!"

"Sorry," I say. What a stupid mistake.

"What are you doing out here?"

I subtly glance back at Jenna's window. Empty now. As if she had never been there. Thank god. I start to lean down for my phone. "Um, I thought I saw some sort of plane in the sky, but it was really bright, so I was trying to take a picture of it, but then –"

She snatches the phone off the ground and hands it over to me. "A UFO?" Rachel snorts.

"Not a UFO!" I say, rolling my eyes.

"Didn't know you were so into conspiracy theories. Do you think the earth is flat too, or –"

I push her playfully on the arm. "Oh, shut up. Let's go inside."

Rachel laughs and grabs me by the arm, leaning her head on me as we walk. "Aw, Chasey. I'm going to miss you."

I can feel her blond baby hair near her scalp tickling my

arm. I remember when Dan and Rachel were born. So tiny, so tender and soft. They'll always be babies to me. I feel a pang of guilt. If Rachel is just a baby to me, shouldn't Jenna be just a baby too?

Once we're inside, I ask Rachel if she wants to have some ice cream with me. She protests at first: "I have to get back to studying. I just came down for a glass of water."

"Oh, come on, you can take a fifteen-minute break and hang out with your big bro, huh?" I say, pulling out the tub of ice cream. "Besides, it's your favorite."

Her eyes narrow. "Is it green?"

I chuckle. Rachel has always insisted mint chocolate chip ice cream tastes different when it's green. "Of course."

She smiles mischievously. "Fine."

She sits with her legs curled up on the kitchen island while I scoop us two mugfuls of ice cream. "So... What's this test you have tomorrow?"

"Applied marketing management," she groans. "I didn't take it during the year and now I'm kicking myself for it."

"Spent too much time partying, huh?" I tease, handing her a mug and a spoon.

"*No*," she retorts and then grumbles a thank you. "Maybe. I don't know. It's hard not to love thirsty Thursdays."

I shake my head. "Wow, my little sister is a party girl, huh?"

Rachel takes a big spoonful of ice cream and rolls her eyes at me. "You're one to talk Mr. 'Trash-the-hotel-room'."

"For the record, no one in our band does that."

"Anyway, it's a four-hour test and it's tomorrow and I'm going to be cramming all night."

I smile at her. She's so grown up now. Maybe I need to get the baby-sister thing out of my head. "And then..."

"And *then* I'm going to celebrate tomorrow night. *Hard*," she says with a big laugh.

We talk a little longer as we eat our ice cream before Rachel has to kick off to finish her studying. "Good luck, sis. You'll kill it tomorrow."

Rachel slips her arms around my waist and gives me a tight hug. "You're the best."

The guilt creeps back in. It feels different now, though. Less like shame, less like I'm a puppy with my tail between my legs. More like...being on the edge of a cliff and knowing I need to jump.

"You're the best," I murmur back and kiss the top of her head.

Once she's upstairs, I'm able to check my phone. A text from Jenna.

*Oops! Close call. Sorry. I'll see you tomorrow.*

Finished with a little silly face. And a heart.

I send a heart back and tuck my phone up against my chest. Yeah...I think I need to jump.

§

I wait for Jenna this morning out on the front stoop. I'm nervous, but not pacing-nervous, not toe-tapping nervously. It's the kind of nervous I get before a show. Grounded and ready. Anticipating that once I get out there, all the nerves are going to wash away once I'm behind the kit and hear the crowd cheering.

Now, there isn't a crowd or a kit this time, but that same exhilaration is brewing inside me. And while this moment has much more of an emotional risk, I know I have to do it. I know I'll regret not doing it.

I've made sure I look the best I can, all things considered. I've trimmed my beard, put gel in my hair, and put on a linen button-up. I want her to know I'm taking this seriously.

"Oh hey!" Jenna cries out with a smile when she sees me outside the house.

I sit up straighter. "Hey."

She walks up the front path, looking cute as ever in a little red dress with a white hibiscus flower pattern hanging off her shoulders by spaghetti straps. Her dark hair is tied back into a waterfall of curls. The whole plane of her clavicle is exposed; I want to kiss her so badly. "What are you doing out here?" she asks.

"Uh..." I've lost my courage. I thought I'd come right out and say it, but it feels impossible now that we're face to face. "It's nice out. You want to sit for a bit?"

Jenna frowns. She knows something is up.

I pat the stair next to me. "Come on, don't be shy."

She sits next to me. I can smell her sweet perfume wafting off her neck. I can't look at her. I focus on my hands which I have clasped between my thighs. "How was your appointment yesterday?" Jenna asks.

"Oh, it was good," I say, except the memory of it stings. "Said I can probably get the cast off in a week."

"That's great!" she says cheerfully.

I swallow. "Yeah, it is great."

"You can play again! That's amazing, Chase," Jenna goes on. "You must be so ready to be..." she trails off. The cogs are turning. No cast means I'm free. No cast means I'm gone. "So ready to get back to your life."

I sigh. "Yeah. I mean, there's a lot to do before we start recording our next album. Got to get my house in order. I bet all my plants are dead."

She giggles. "I didn't know you were a plant dad."

"Barely," I chuckle in reply.

We are both quiet. I can feel her eyes on me, waiting for

me to look at her, trying to figure out what's in my head. My heart is pounding so hard I can hear my blood rushing in my ears. Fuck, I need to say it.

"Something on your mind?"

I smile to myself. Jenna can tell. She always can. We're so fucking in synch. Or she cares an awful lot. I take a deep breath. "Yeah, I do have...something on my mind..." I reach for her hand and grab it.

"Chase, someone might see," she whispers, trying to pull her hand away.

"I don't care," I say firmly.

Jenna looks at me. Her woody, hazel eyes are widened, lashes curled upward to the heavens. So confused and innocent.

I squeeze her hand and gently pull it into my lap, engulfing our grip with my other hand. "Listen to me," I say. My voice comes out smaller than expected, in a way I don't share with most people. "I don't...I don't want this to end."

She smiles sadly. "I know, me either."

"No, I don't mean – I don't mean, 'Let's make this time count.' I mean..." I lean closer to her. "I mean, *I don't want this to end*."

Jenna's lips part as my words hit her.

"I want to..." *Say it, Chase. Fucking say it.* "I want to be with you, Jenna."

Her eyebrows jump. I'm not sure if with surprise or if I've upset her.

"I don't want to sneak around. I don't want us to be a dirty, little secret," I say. Emotion creeps into my voice. "I know that I want you. And I think we should give us a chance. Perhaps it's ridiculous...maybe a little crazy, but –"

I don't get a chance to finish before Jenna's lips are on mine in a deep kiss. My nerves immediately settle and I gasp in surprise against her lips. She touches my chest and I encircle my arms around her. No words could have made her answer clearer.

Jenna draws away, puts her hands on my face. There are tears in her eyes. "You are crazy. This is crazy and I...I want to be with you too." She blinks, letting swollen teardrops rush down her face. "Or at least to try. So bad."

I wipe the tears away with my thumb. "Don't cry, Jens, don't cry."

"I can't help it, I'm just so happy," she says, her voice breaking with laughter. "I'm so, so happy."

I start laughing too. This couldn't have gone better. I kiss her again, more chaste this time. I've never felt so bonded to someone like this. So...in love, maybe. "Hey," I whisper after the kiss parts. "I'm kissing you on the front steps."

Jenna looks askance to the neighborhood, a blush across her cheeks. Then, she smiles giddily. "You're kissing me on the front steps."

"The whole world can see," I say with a proud smile on my face.

"So...how do we tell everyone?"

My stomach drops.

"Oh god, how do we tell Rachel?" Jenna says, her lips curling up with dread.

I wave off the thought. "We'll figure that out. Together."

Her hand intertwines with mine and she brings it up to her chest, holding it to her dearly. "I like the sound of that."

There's a lot in our way. Our lives are so different. I can't even imagine how we will align them. But I can't imagine not being with her. At least not *trying* to be with her. I wrap my arm around her shoulder and pull her into me. We look out at the front lawn, onto the open street. A car passes by and the driver raises their hand in a greeting, the way we do around the neighborhood. We both wave back and then exchange a look.

"No going back now..." I say, squeezing her waist.

"Yes, I'm sure they'll be posting about it on the neighborhood watch Facebook group in mere minutes."

We both laugh and sit there in the glow of our admissions for a few more minutes.

"How do we celebrate?" Jenna asks eventually.

"You're in luck. I think there's a bottle of champagne somewhere in the liquor cabinet I can scrounge up for us..."

Jenna's hand creeps up my thigh. "I had something else in mind..."

She doesn't have to tell me twice. I practically haul her over my shoulder inside. Someone should call me the bionic man because the feats I've accomplished with just one leg are out of this world. We disrobe eagerly, Jenna unbuttoning my pants, me sliding her dress up her thighs. Our lips reach for each other, again and again, in a deep dance of tongues. There's no way we could be closer to each other and yet we try.

"Lay back," Jenna instructs, pushing me down onto the couch lengthwise. "I want to do something for you."

And before I can even ask, Jenna's wrapping her lips around the head of my cock. I pant in surprise. "God, Jenna."

Her tongue swirls around me as she pushes her mouth further and further down my length. Each pulse of her lips feels like heaven. Jenna rises her eyes up to me and bats her lashes almost innocently. I laugh, but it turns into a whimper when I feel my cock hit the back of her throat. Jenna moans, sending vibrations through me. I have to grab onto the back of the couch for support as my head falls back and my eyes flutter shut.

"Fuck, Jenna, your mouth feels so good."

She hums happily. A buzz of pleasure spreads out through my pelvis. I start to rock my hips up toward her mouth gently. Clearly, she makes up for her inexperience with her enthusiasm. With a free hand, she caresses my balls, pressing at the base of my cock with her thumb. My whole body shudders.

"If you keep doing that, I'm going to..."

Jenna releases me from her mouth, keeping the head up against her lips. "Where do you want to come, baby?"

"Inside. Inside, I want to come –" Jenna licks my cock from base to tip slowly and my eyes roll back. "Fuuuck, Jenna, come ride me."

She smiles and straddles me, teasing my cock with her pussy. She's wet, practically dripping. I put my hands on her hips, guiding her back and forth over me so I can recalibrate. I don't want to come too fast.

"Hair up or down?" Jenna asks, tossing her ponytail to the side.

"Down, take it down."

She pulls the ponytail holder out of her hair; it tumbles down over her shoulders, giving her a wild, hungry look.

"You're so beautiful, Jens. So beautiful," I murmur.

Jenna wraps her hand around my cock and puts the head up against her entrance. I shift my hips forward and feel myself dip inside her honeypot. Her breath shifts. "Go slow..."

"You're in control. Use me, baby," I say, leaning up and running my hands up and down her back. "Use me."

Jenna nods, her head tilting back. She slowly slides up and down my cock, figuring out her rhythm. I look at the place where we meet, the beautiful way we intertwine. I can't help but be gleeful that I get to do this for longer than a week, hopefully much longer.

"Good girl," I croon.

Jenna grunts in response. Her speed increases, sending shocks down my body with each thrust. "Oh my god, baby."

"You feel good?"

She nods, gluing her hands to my shoulders for leverage. Up close, she almost looks like she's in pain. Her mouth drops open and a thrumming, long groan comes out as she forces me deep inside her.

I squeeze her ass in my hands. "Yes, baby, that's it."

Her groan continues.

"You want some help?"

She nods heavily. Words are escaping her

"Come here." I wrap my arms around her, draw her chest to mine, feel her full breasts press against my chest, and begin to thrust up, deep inside of her.

Jenna takes all of me so well, mewling into my neck desperately. She presses her face into my neck. "Chase... Chase...you make me feel so good." She repeats my name like it's a magical incantation.

I feel my orgasm building, like a rubber band being tightened and tightened, knowing it will eventually snap.

"You're my girl, Jenna. You're going to be my girl."

"I'm your girl," she moans loudly. "I'm your girl."

I tighten my lips together and give one, two, three more strokes, each one like turning up the volume on the stereo until it can't get any louder. I press myself as deep as I can go, revel in her curdled cry, and explode.

Jenna follows me, her pussy tightening around me. I curse into her hair as I am bathed in the euphoria of my orgasm, the snapping rubber band. I hold her tight to me, so tight I'm afraid I'm hurting her. But I can't let her go. I won't let her go now. Or ever, maybe.

Jenna lifts her hips slightly and then slams back down on me, giving one last pulse of pleasure to both of us. I cup her ass in my hand and rub it gingerly. "You're my girl," I say in her ear.

She sighs contentedly and rests her head on my chest. I stroke her hair gently, kiss her forehead. I could get used to this.

Our reverie doesn't last long because only minutes after we've finished, we hear the jangling of keys in the door. We look at each other with horror.

Jenna leaps off of me and grabs her dress. "Chase! Who is that??"

"I don't know, I don't –" I start to sit up. I'm totally naked and can't reach my pants – they're strewn over the armchair. "Jenna, my pants."

She lunges for the pants and tosses them to me, but it's too late. The front door swings open. I cover myself with my pants.

Rachel stands in the doorway, frozen, her keys still dangling from the door. "What the fuck?"

Jenna runs her hands back through her hair. "Hi, Rach."

Rachel's eyes jump from Jenna to me; she recoils once she sees I'm mostly unclothed. "Jesus Christ, Chase, what the fuck!"

"Sorry, I –"

"Why are you *naked???*" she screeches, her hands over her eyes.

"What are you doing home?!"

"I finished my exam early! *Put your pants on!*"

"We can explain," Jenna says, going over to Rachel while I try and wriggle my pants on.

Rachel comes into the house, her hands still plastered to her eyes. "Oh my god, oh my god, *oh my fucking god.*"

This couldn't be a worse situation. Once my pants are haphazardly on, I reach for my shirt on the ground. "Rachel, please, calm down and –"

"Calm *DOWN?!*" she screams, spinning around toward me. Her hands are now gripped in fists at her sides. And her eyes...Jesus, a look so cold she could turn me to ice. "Don't you dare tell me to calm down."

The room falls silent. I try to button up my shirt, but my hands are shaking. Jenna stands in the corner of the room near the window, as far from me as possible. I plead to her silently *Look at me, look at me, look at me.* She won't, though. She can't.

"I need a drink," Rachel mumbles. She disappears into the kitchen. We hear the snap of a can tab. She returns holding a White Claw; she guzzles it down and then gives us that icy stare again. "How long has this been going on?"

Jenna purses her lips and crosses her arms over her chest.

"Almost a month," I say as confidently as I can.

Rachel's eyes bug out. "A month? A whole fucking month???"

"Rachel, please stop yelling," Jenna says quietly. "Let's sit and talk and –"

"You're fucking kidding, right?" Rachel spits back. "I'm not going to sit and talk with you after I've – oh my god. I should have known, I should have seen it."

I clear my throat. "Please let us explain –"

"I don't care," she says, pinching her nose bridge as if I'm an annoying fly in her ear. "I don't want the details. This is so unhinged. How could you do that to me? She's my best friend."

"Listen, Rach –" Jenna starts.

Rachel cuts her off even before she can begin, approaching her like a feral cat. "No, you listen. I trusted you. I asked you to come over here and see my brother and, I don't know, hang out? Play monopoly? Not to…" She trails off and her anger fades. "How could you? And when I asked you why you were ditching me all summer? Why wouldn't you tell me? You had every chance and you still lied to me."

Jenna shakes her head. "Rachel, I felt so guilty, I just –" She moves toward her and touches Rachel's arm, but Rachel jerks her arm away.

*"Don't touch me."*

"Rachel, please…she didn't mean to hurt you. *We* didn't," I feel my jaw tighten. "We didn't mean to –"

"'We'?" Rachel repeats with disgust. "As long as there is a 'we' between the two of you, you can count me out. Because this…" She looks to each of us, anger and hurt blatant on her face. "I'll *never* be okay with this."

I start to say something, but Rachel tears off upstairs to her room. Her door slams loudly, and the harshest silence falls back over the house.

Jenna folds her hands over her face and begins to cry.

"Jens…" I say. I get to my feet awkwardly and prop my crutches under my arms. "Please, don't cry, she's…" I make my way over to her. "She's being dramatic. She just needs some time to calm down and –"

"No," Jenna says, her voice pregnant with sobs. "No, this was – we knew we shouldn't and we did anyway. That was selfish of us." She looks up at me; her face is glossy with tears. "We should never have done it, Chase. This… We… I'm sorry, but I can't."

If Rachel had stabbed me in the gut, Jenna has twisted

the knife. How could everything have fallen apart so quickly? We were supposed to give us a shot and now she wants to pretend we never existed before our time is even up.

"I have to go." She runs for the front door.

"Jenna, wait –"

I can't move quickly enough to catch up with her, and in the blink of an eye, she's disappeared out the door and down the walk. I stand there, staring, as if I'm watching the ghost of her leaving on repeat, her hair bouncing over her shoulders and her unlaced sandals thwapping. And I already feel her absence inside my chest.

12

———

JENNA

I RUSH INSIDE AND UP TO MY ROOM, TEARS STREAMING down my face. This was all a mistake from the beginning. I should have visited Chase that first day and been done with it. I should have known I wouldn't be able to help myself and it would go too far.

I lie in bed with the guilt heavy on my chest and mind, the shame of being discovered, the fear of what's to come. If Chase and I had just gone with the plan, things would have been over in a week and maybe Rachel never would have known. Now I've lost *both* of them.

I cry until I fall asleep. By the time I wake up, twilight is creeping over the sky. I check my phone. No messages. That somehow makes it worse. I thought maybe Chase would reach out or Rachel would...I don't know, calm down. She usually can't hold a grudge no matter how angry she is. When someone crosses her, she'll talk a big game in private, say absolutely scathing things about people until it is all out of her system, and when she sees them next, she talks to them like she's their best friend. I've always admired that in her. Her ability to forgive.

I guess that ability stops when it comes to me.

I can't blame her. She must feel so betrayed. But if I could just explain to her, once she's cooled off, maybe she would understand why it happened. And I could tell her that Chase and I are no longer...

I feel a pain deep in my head. The onset of a migraine. I've only had a few in my life, but fuck, I know one when I feel one. The light from my phone makes the dull ache even worse. I'll just send a text and be done with it, check my phone later, maybe after I eat something.

*Rach – I'm so sorry I didn't tell you. It's over now, I promise. Could we talk IRL so I can explain how it happened and apologize?*

Shockingly, the telltale three dots appear almost immediately. I stare at the phone, waiting, waiting. They disappear. My heart sinks. They reappear. I wait...and wait. This can't be good. She's taking too long. She's either trying to make something not sound too mean or trying to make it sound as mean as possible.

I'll accept it. I deserve it. She can be as mad as she wants. I just want my friend back.

Abruptly, a message appears.

*I don't want to talk. Stay away from me and my family.*

Somehow, for all the worst-case scenarios that ran through my head, this is even worse. I drop my phone out of complete shock. Is this what twenty-one years boils down to? *Stay away?*

I don't deserve to cry. I brought this all on myself. I sink into self-flagellating and count up all my failings. No job, no internship, no friends, no boyfriend...I'm a fucking loser. I've said it from the beginning of the summer.

I'm a loser.

Just then, mom knocks on my door. "Jenna? Dinner's ready."

I am not hungry. Not at all. My stomach feels like one big knot, like I've swallowed a whole pack of gum. "I'm not hungry tonight. I'm sorry."

She pauses. "Is everything alright?"

"I'm just not feeling well," I say, another crop of tears starts trembling in my eyes.

"Then you should eat," she says sweetly.

I pause. How can I face them after all of this? I'm not good at hiding the truth from them. Never have been. This would just be too much. "Maybe later."

My mom doesn't push. She's good about that. Always lets me come around in my own time.

I fall back into a coma of sorrow, not sure if I'm sleeping or just in a waking nightmare. When I come to again, it's dark out. Downstairs, the television is on and my parents are laughing from time to time, talking. They're so cute together. They have their shows they won't watch without each other.

I finally pull myself from the bed, wrap myself in a blanket, and trudge heavily downstairs.

"There you are, honey," Mom greets me with a soft smile from her place on the couch. "What's going on?"

I shake my head. "I don't want to talk about it."

They exchange a worried look, but again, don't push. Dad waves me into the room. "Come watch with us."

I look at the TV. It's some singing reality competition. There are so many nowadays, it's hard to keep track of them. I go sit next to Mom on the couch, pulling my legs up to my chest. The show isn't really that interesting to me. It's just nice to not be alone.

Without another word, my Mom touches my shoulder

and gently guides me down so my head is resting on her lap. She strokes my hair.

I am still deserving of softness. I might have hurt Rachel, but I am still deserving of love and softness. I curl up into her and press my face to her thigh. At least I can feel safe here. Even if everything else has fallen apart.

13

———

## CHASE

"Rachel! Dinner!" Mom calls up the stairs, red in the face from shouting. She's called her down about three times already. She comes into the dining room with an incredulous look on her face. "What's wrong with her?"

I bite my lip.

"Dan, go upstairs and get your sister," Dad says to Dan who has already started gnawing on an ear of corn.

"Come on, Dad. Why do I have to do it? I just sat down for the first time all day," he moans.

Dad scoffs, "Because you're not old like the rest of us!"

"Hey!" I say defensively.

"Or...incapacitated," Dad corrects with a gesture to my leg.

Dan sighs and pushes himself up from his seat, but I stop him. "She's not coming down."

They all look at me. "What did you say, honey?" Mom asks.

"She's..." I take a deep breath. "She's not coming down. Because she's mad at me."

Mom frowns. "What is she mad at you about?"

I scan their faces. Mom and Dad both have expressions of concern while Dan just looks utterly confused. I need to fix things. And they need to hear the story from my side before Rachel gets in their ear. "Dan, could you give us a moment?"

"What's going on, kiddo?" Dad asks, his brow knotted at the center.

I swallow. Better rip it off like a bandage. "Rachel's mad at me because I've been...I've been seeing Jenna."

They look at me bewilderedly.

"In a...in a romantic way," I add.

My mother's eyes widen, big blue plunging ponds. "What?"

"I thought she was just – I thought she was keeping you company," Dad stumbles over his words. "Not keeping you *company*."

"Ed..." Mom admonishes him.

I shake my head. "It's not like that. And it wasn't...we tried to be just friends, but it became clear we saw each other as more than that."

"Well, honey, she's so young," Mom says, concern in her voice.

"I know."

"And she's still in school," Dad follows up firmly.

"And she's Rachel's best friend! She's just a kid still."

"Hey." It's Dan's turn to feel indignant about their age-related stabs at us. And I have to agree with him.

"She's not. She's not just a kid. I thought that at first too, but she's...Jenna's mature, and she's grounded and so smart and..." I remember how she ran out. How she left me standing there. "We knew no one would really understand. So we kept it a secret, thought it would just be a fling until I got my cast off and moved back home. But when we figured out our feelings were mutual –"

Mom interjects. "What kind of feelings?"

I feel a swell of happiness inside. "Deep feelings, Ma. Like –" I can't say love. My parents can't know I love Jenna before she does. Because that's what I feel for her. *Love*. So much love. I can't lose her.

In my silence, Dad speaks, "Wow, Chase." His voice is gentle. It's like he knows what I want to say. Like he's been in my exact shoes.

I nod. "We shouldn't have hidden it. We should have just been honest. Rachel walked in on us today and she...I don't blame her for feeling hurt. That we've betrayed her trust. But..."

Mom reaches out and takes my hand. Her eyes twinkle. "Oh, Chase. She'll forgive you."

"But do you understand? I know Jenna's young, but she's..." I get the memory of Jenna lying on my chest on the couch, before everything went sour. "She's my girl."

Mom and Dad look at each other and share a smile. All their years together passing between them. Their high school prom, their wedding, my birth, all the years of trying for Rachel and Dan, showing up to my gigs as they got bigger and bigger, dinner with all of their grown children. They get it. I know they do.

"Just take good care of her," Mom says softly.

"I will." If she'll talk to me again...

"Rachel will come around, just give her some time," Dad adds. "She can be a tough cookie."

Tears on his face, looking at his (mostly empty now) dinner plate, Dan says, "Man, that's so beautiful."

I can't help but laugh. For being the hardened, cool football player, Dan's always had a little soft spot.

"I'm so happy for you. Jenna's perfect for you," he adds and then tearfully eats a forkful of potatoes.

At least one of the twins is on board.

Later, when I'm alone in bed, I text Jenna.

*Talked to my parents about us. They're cool with it. Better than cool. :) I know you're upset, but please text me, baby. I want to work this out.*

I get no response that night. I have a fitful night of sleep and wake up to...no text back in the morning either.

It doesn't help that things are enormously tense in the MacAllistair house. Rachel won't even look at me, won't acknowledge my presence. Mom and Dad scold her and Dan tries to make her acknowledge me, but she stonewalls us all. Fuck, this is going to be difficult.

The week passes silently. Jenna doesn't reach out and Rachel plays her role of ice queen to perfection. The only times I see Jenna are when she goes on a morning run, but she always sprints past our house, her head down.

Something has to change.

Luckily, at the end of the week, my appointment with my doctor comes along and, lo and behold, the cast is ready to come off. "The bone is almost as good as new," he announces almost cheerfully when I get to my feet. "You'll still have to use your crutches for a while and have your PT sessions. We need to make sure it's all perfect before we put any extra weight on that leg."

I don't care that I have to wear the damn crutches still. Despite a woozy feeling in my left leg, I am filled with confidence now that I'm able to stand on my own two feet again. I'm Chase MacAllistair, dammit. I'm a drummer again.

I have Jay drive me home as fast as he can; I'm so eager to get into the basement and play on my old kit. Work out some of the ideas that have been building in my head. But as soon as I'm standing on the front walk and Jay drives off, my heart pulls me in a different direction. I walk next door to the O'Donnell house with measured purpose, easily now that the cast isn't weighing me down and that I can start putting a bit of pressure on my foot. I walk up the front walk, the porch stairs, to their neatly painted blue door.

I'm not sure what I'm trying to do. I just need something to change. I ring the doorbell. There's no response. I look over my shoulder. Jenna's car isn't parked in the driveway like it normally is. Which probably means no one is home, since her parents both work during the day and –

The front door opens suddenly. Jenna's dad. "Chase! What are you doing here?"

"Hi Mr. O'Donnell," I say. "Is Jenna home?"

Mr. O'Donnell's dark brows furrow. "No, she's out shopping, I believe."

"Oh." My mouth is dry. "I'm sorry, I didn't realize you'd be here, I just –"

"I'm working from home today," he replies. There's skepticism in his voice. "Can I help you with something?"

Now or never. Just like it's been ever since Jenna walked into my life. "I'd like to talk to you about something. You mind if I come in?"

Mr. O'Donnell's skepticism does not fade until we are sitting across from one another at his desk like it's a job interview and I spill my guts to him. "I want to be with your daughter."

He looks at me in total shock. "I beg your pardon?"

"We've been seeing each other, and even though it hasn't been very long, I'm confident that she's someone I want in my life for a long time. Perhaps forever," I say. God, I'm going to have such a vulnerability hangover after this.

"Aren't you a little old for her?" Mr. O'Donnell asks, edginess percolating in his words.

I nod. "Yes, but we've...we're both aware of the challenge that may bring. And if we could have helped it, we would have. But I think Jenna and I see each other beyond our age. We've connected on a very deep level, Mr. O'Donnell."

He stares at me, unspeaking.

"And while I know perhaps I'm not the ideal candidate you would want for your daughter, I can provide for her," I say. "I'll give her the best life she could possibly have."

Mr. O'Donnell considers this, resting his hand on his chin. "She'd need to finish school first."

"Yes, I wouldn't dream of taking her away from that."

"And my wife would have to be alright with it."

I smile. "Absolutely. I would be happy to talk with Mrs. O'Donnell."

"And most importantly...Jenna would have to want a life with you, too," Mr. O'Donnell says. It is clear that he is a father who has raised a strong young woman who should not compromise on anything to be with a man.

And that's what I love about her. "Of course. More important than anything."

Mr. O'Donnell whips out his phone. I'm confused until I hear him greet the person on the line. "Kathy, honey, I have a young man here who has something he'd like to ask you."

*Now?* I mouth to him as he hands the phone over to me.

He shrugs and puts it on speakerphone. "Why wait?"

I take the phone and greet Mrs. O'Donnell before explaining the whole situation to her. And, to my surprise, she is ecstatic, giggling and celebrating. "I knew Jenna was lovesick, I could just tell," she announces.

"Yes, about that –" I reply, concocting a plan in my head. "Perhaps you and Mr. O'Donnell could help me plan something special for Jenna. I want to make sure it's perfect and I don't know who better to help me than her parents."

Mr. O'Donnell smiles at me as Mrs. O'Donnell enthusiastically replies, "*Yes*, of course. Anything you need, Chase MacAllistair."

WHEN I RETURN HOME, I GO STRAIGHT TO THE basement and release all the nerves into my drumkit. It's been so stressful having to reveal my heart over and over again to people who aren't even Jenna.

I know there is a possibility Jenna is really, truly done with me. That things have been ruined beyond repair. I can only hope that this special night I'm going to put together can fix things.

But I know there's one thing more important than that.

When Rachel walks in from school at four pm on the dot, I make my way upstairs. Though still wearing crutches, it is nice to be able to go up and down stairs more easily. It's so nice to be free again. I don't care if I'm pushing myself too hard. I go right up to her room, where the door is ajar and knock. "Rach?"

Any movement in the room stills.

"I know you're in there Rachel. Can we talk?"

She doesn't respond.

"I'm going to come in unless you say something to me in three...two..."

"Come in," Rachel says in a cool voice.

I push open the door and find Rachel sitting at the head of her bed, tucked into the corner of the room. She still has her makeup on from the day which makes her look even more intimidating. When she sees me, her eyes widen. I can tell she's surprised to see me with my cast off but is too upset with me to say anything.

"Can I sit?" I ask, pointing to her plush pink desk chair at the white desk by the window.

Rachel raises her eyebrows expectantly. *Obviously*.

"Thanks," I say in a small voice. I go to sit; I feel a little too big for the chair.

"Well?"

I swallow. "I want to explain what's going on."

She rolls her eyes. "I'm not eight, Chase."

"Really? I mean, I know, that's not what I..." I clasp my hands between my knees. "Okay. Sorry. Bad start."

"Yeah," Rachel says with a scathing look in her eyes.

I take a deep breath. "I'm so sorry I betrayed your trust."

Her face softens the slightest bit.

"I can only imagine how painful that must have been to walk in on. I know it looked a certain way and all I can say is sorry now that I've hurt you."

Rachel takes a heart-shaped decorative pillow and puts it on her lap. It makes her look so small. "Tell me how it happened," she says quietly.

"Well...it started before it really started," I reply. "You have to understand, Rach, I'm getting older. And I've been around the block."

"Mhm," she says with judgment on her lips.

"Which is to say," I go on, "the moment I saw Jenna, I knew there was something different about her. I just knew in my gut that...she was someone special. And I tried to resist that feeling, I really did. I tried to set aside my feelings and just be friends with her. But it caught up to me, my feelings got too big to manage. And she felt the same."

Rachel's woundedness is apparent on her face.

"So, we thought we could keep it a secret and just enjoy each other's company until we went our separate ways, but then we both realized it's deeper than that. It's more than that. I care for her. I want to be with her." My breath catches. "I love her, Rachel."

Her eyes widen.

"I know that's hard to believe. And a little weird since I'm older and your brother."

"You can say that again."

I nod. "I'm sorry I didn't let you in...didn't let you see it as it was happening. It must feel so out of the blue."

The hardness in Rachel's face breaks and suddenly she's crying. She leaps off the bed and wraps her arms around me. "I'm so mad at you," she sobs into my shoulder.

I can't help but chuckle just a little bit. "I know, I'm sorry, Rach."

"I can't believe you fell in love with my best friend."

"You have good taste in friends, what can I say?"

Rachel draws back and wipes her face with the backs of her hands. "Does she love you back?"

I sigh. "I don't know. She hasn't spoken to me since. Won't respond to my texts."

"Mm," she says, pouting her lips. "That's my fault. I told her to leave you alone."

"Rachel..." I admonish.

"I was mad at you guys! Still am, by the way," she grunts.

I smile sullenly. "I'll make it up to you. I promise."

Rachel is quiet. She considers me with narrowed eyes. "I want you to be happy. But you can't hurt her."

"Wouldn't dream of it."

She hugs me again. I pull her into me tight, as tight as

can be. When she was little, she used to ask for Chase hugs, and when I started going on tour, she would be beside herself sometimes asking for me. I know I can't baby her anymore. She's a young woman now. But she'll always fit right in my arms like she did when she was four years old.

"I love you, Rach. You know I do."

"I love you too." She smacks my knee. "And your leg!"

"I know!"

"Do a little walk for me, I want to see!"

"Just a couple of steps. I'm not supposed to be off my crutches just yet." But I still get up and walk around the room, pretending to toss my hair. She giggles.

"How does it feel?"

"Great! So great," I say, running a hand through my hair. "But listen, I need your help with something."

Rachel crosses her arms. "You need my *help*?"

"I know, I know. I'll owe you twice as much after this," I say and sit next to her on the bed. "I'm trying to plan a special night for Jenna. We can make amends and clear the air. Maybe...rekindle what we've started."

"Ew," she says playfully.

"Shut up," I laugh. "But I'll need to make sure she's out of the house. Distracted. Do you think maybe you can be in charge of that?"

Rachel nods slowly and looks up at the ceiling, thinking. "Spa day."

"Yes. That's perfect."

She grins. "And you're paying."

I sigh. "Yes, ma'am."

## 14

## JENNA

"JENNA! RACHEL'S AT THE DOOR FOR YOU!"

I sit stock straight up in bed. I've been sleeping in later these days. At least when I'm sleeping, I can escape from reality.

"Jenna!"

I jump out of bed, still in my pajamas, and rush down the stairs. I have replayed this moment in my head, when Rachel finally, finally feels ready to forgive me. In my head, I was a lot cooler about it. Not as eager as this. But I can't help it. I'm ready to talk. I've missed her.

I breeze past my mom in the front hallway and go right onto the porch. Rachel sits on the porch swing, kicking her feet cheerfully. "Hey, Jens."

I stare at her. "Hey."

"Oh, shit, you're not dressed."

I look down at my pajamas. "Uh. Yeah. I just woke up."

"Okay, well, we have plans, so go put some clothes on."

I frown. "What?"

"Doesn't matter what you wear. Just go put something on that you won't feel embarrassed to wear in public."

"Rach, what are you –"

"Don't ask, I'm not answering. Now get going."

I have no idea what's going on right now, but I don't care. Rachel is here and she wants to spend time with me, so I follow her instructions in a flurry, almost forgetting my purse on the way out the door. Rachel looks me up and down. "That'll do. Now come on."

We get into her mom's car which she's borrowed for the day. At first, the ride is silent, except for the radio playing some poppy top 40. Every muscle in my body is tense as can be.

"Where are we going?" I finally ask.

"Well," she starts, tossing her hair over her shoulder. "I feel a little bad for how I handled everything so I thought maybe we could have a spa day and relax and maybe hash everything out."

I raise my eyebrows. "Oh. That's really nice."

"I know, right?" Rachel says with a grin. I'm glad she's still willing to be playful with me.

"I don't really have the money for a spa –"

"It's taken care of. My treat."

I frown. It's awfully generous, but I'm not sure what I did to deserve this, especially after she was so clear that I stay away from the MacAllistairs. Away from Chase.

I've been thinking about Chase pretty much nonstop. I sometimes look out my window to try and catch glimpses of him on the deck or in the yard. It's a compulsion. I have to do it, have to get a glimpse of him. I have to know if he's okay without me. Of course, I can't get a read on him from that far away, not to mention he's probably trying to shove everything under the surface too to make sure everything is normal at home.

I think it's better for me if I just pretend none of it was real. We'll go our separate ways as planned. And maybe life will go back to normal.

We get to the spa and are immediately whisked into a massage room. A "couples" massage, which Rachel laughs about, pointing to the rose petals strewn across the room. We exchange pleasant conversations from time to time while we are massaged from head to toe. Turns out I *really* needed a massage. My whole body feels lighter than air once I get off the table. Then, they send us to a different room where we are given rejuvenating facials that prickle my cheeks in the best way. They guide us into the thermal baths to wait out our facials, which are housed in a beautiful room with lofty ceilings, exposed brick, and rafters. The lighting is low, nearly romantic.

"Oh, I needed this," Rachel sighs as she steps into the warm, steaming water.

I follow her and understand immediately. It consumes me in the best way. I feel transported away from the stress and depression as the water wraps around me. I feel so safe, even with Rachel nearby, with the beginnings of a hard conversation percolating between us.

"So..." she begins.

I look over at her and can't help but snort in laughter.

"What?"

"Just hard to take you seriously with your face all green and –"

"Your face is all green too!" she shoots back.

We laugh. One of the attendants stops by with glasses of red wine. "This is the real deal," I say. I wonder again how she's paid for this. This isn't just a mani/pedi day. This is *luxe.*

"Anyway," Rachel begins again, "I just want to apologize for the way I handled...everything."

I almost spit out my wine. *She's* apologizing to *me*? "I'm sorry too, Rach. You know I would never want to hurt you, I just –"

"I know that what's between you two is real," she cuts me off. Even though her face looks ridiculous, I can see the seriousness in her eyes. Blue like the water. Like her brother's. "But I'm upset I found out the way I did. And I'm upset you didn't tell me."

How could she possibly know it's real? We haven't spoken in days. Unless she and Chase... "I regret not telling you."

"I just thought we told each other everything, you know?"

"And we do," I say, sloshing through the water closer to her.

"But you didn't. You didn't tell me this really, really important thing."

I look down into my wine.

"Like arguably one of the *most important* things."

I sighed. "I was trying to protect you. I know it doesn't feel like it -"

"No, Jenna. You were trying to protect *you*."

My stomach flips; our eyes meet. She's not angry. She's just firm. And she's correct. "You're right. I'm sorry. I...knew it was wrong and I didn't want to upset you."

"Do you really think it was wrong?"

"Oh yeah. Obviously, I mean. That went about as poorly as it could have with the way you found out," I half-laugh. I'm struck with the memory of Chase and me sitting on their front steps, deciding we were going to try this for real.

"So you don't really like him?"

This feels like a trap, and I navigate it as such. "I mean, of course, I like him."

"But do you like-like him?"

"Jeez, Rach, that's so middle school."

She raises an eyebrow. "Answer the question."

I hesitate. I don't know what she wants to hear. But I've already lied enough to her. I've already pushed the trust in our friendship to the brink of almost disrepair. What would be the point of lying anymore? "Um...yeah. Yeah, I do like-like him."

To my surprise, Rachel smiles at me and nods as if she knew that was my answer.

"It wasn't supposed to –"

"Stop," Rachel cuts me off with a laugh. "Stop trying to explain it, Jenna."

I screw my lips together. "It doesn't matter anyway because it's over. We're done, Rachel. You can be sure of that."

"Do you want to be done?"

I huff. My heart is racing with anxiety. I put my wine glass down on the pool's edge and lean over my arms.

"If I gave you my blessing, would you still want to be done?"

I stand up straight suddenly and look at her bewildered. "What?"

Rachel smiles softly. "I talked to Chase yesterday, and from what he said, it sounds like what's between the two of you is really real."

My eyes fill with tears. Could this be real? Could he really still be thinking of me? Still want me?

"Don't get me wrong, I'm hurt that you guys went

behind my back. But that's something I can get over if you two are really happy together. If it's not just –"

"It's not," I say before she even finishes her sentence. "It's not, it's..." I put my hand to my heart. "I really care for him, Rachel."

Rachel grins and reaches out her hand to me. I take it and she pulls me into her suddenly. I laugh as the water splashes up around us. We hug tightly. "It's been so hard to take you seriously with all that schmutz on your face."

We both laugh. It is rather ridiculous to realize that throughout this whole conversation we were both green-faced.

"You have to promise me something, though," she says, pulling back with her hands on her hips.

"Anything! I owe you to the umpteenth degree!"

"That I'll be the maid of honor at your wedding."

My entire body flushes. "Rachel! Don't get ahead of the situation, we haven't even –"

"Promise me!" she says and holds her pinky up.

I wrap my pinky around hers and smile. "Promise."

"And I better be the godmother for your babies."

"*Rachel!!!*"

The rest of the day goes by in a flurry. We finish up our soak, get our facials removed, and admire our baby soft skin in the mirror before having a lush lunch with champagne and charcuterie. The post-lunch activities are filled with glamour including manicures and pedicures and hair stylings to boot. The day is capped off with Rachel and me getting our makeup done. I laugh when the artist asks where I'm going after this. "Probably to dinner with my parents and an episode of *Jeopardy*."

It's late in the day once we finish up, already five

o'clock. Rachel and I shuffle into the car and I get a sinking feeling as we drive off. I'm so grateful we've worked things out between us, but I still have the issue of Chase to actually deal with. I open my phone and look at our text messages, stare at the message I left unanswered, and then type something out.

*Talked with Rachel. Maybe we can talk tonight or tomorrow? I'm sorry. I miss you.*

I don't send it, just stare at my phone thinking about the repercussions of it.

"Send it," Rachel says abruptly.

I look up. "What?"

"You're texting Chase, aren't you?" she asks. "*Send it.*"

"Do you think he's really –"

"I *know* he's really," she giggles.

I look at the message again. Delete the 'I miss you'. "I think I really hurt him."

"Oh my god, Jenna!" Rachel yelps. "Just text the man."

"You say that like it's so easy!"

"It is! It's so easy. You just press that little blue arrow and –"

"I know you're trying to be funny, but it's not funny to me," I say, my hand tightening around my phone.

She turns her eyes from the road. "Jenna, look at me."

"You keep your eyes on the road," I laugh.

"Look at me!"

I do.

Rachel smiles at me; I remember that I'm dear to her. That our friendship, our bond is so deep. We will get past this hurt. "He wants to hear from you. Okay?"

A car horn honks and Rachel jerks the car back into our lane.

"Jesus Christ!"

"I told you to –"

"Oh, shut up!"

We laugh; it was a close call, but we made it. I look back at my phone and retype out, 'I miss you.'

And then, I hit send.

## 15

## CHASE

*Talked with Rachel. Maybe we can talk tonight or tomorrow? I'm sorry. I miss you.*

My heart thumps wildly as I reread the message. She misses me. She misses me and she's willing to give me a chance. Thank god things went well with Rachel. Otherwise, this whole night would have been a bust.

"Chase, which tablecloth?" my dad asks, holding up two similarly cream-toned tablecloths.

I tuck my phone back into my pocket. "They look the same to me," I say.

He scoffs. "Well, they're not! Your mother taught me this color is called eggshell and this one is something like ecru!"

"Father." I touch his shoulder gently. "I trust your judgment."

Dad rolls his eyes. "I just want it to be perfect, Chasey."

"It will be, with your touch!"

He likes the sound of that and makes his way down the stairs of the deck to the yard where Mr. O'Donnell is wiping down a small glass table. All afternoon, these two have been helping me set up and decorate for tonight. There are beautiful twinkling lights strung up from the deck to the fence and bunches of beautiful flowers that Mr. O'Donnell got from his florist friend. Huge sunflowers and green chrysanthemums. It's perfect.

I watch the two of them unfold the tablecloth (described as "ecru," whatever that is) and buoyantly spread it out over the table. The two of them have been chattering all day, more romantic and excited than I ever could have imagined.

Dan walks up the side of the house and into the yard with two chairs over his shoulders. "Where do you want these?"

"Where do you think?" Dad says wryly and gestures to the table.

I turn around and slip inside through the glass sliding door to check on the food. Mom and Mrs. O'Donnell were adamant they be in charge of that. They move through the kitchen with grace and ease, a well-choreographed dance. And the kitchen is remarkably clean for being the midst of cooking. I guess that's a mother's touch. "They're on their way," I announce.

"ETA?" Mom asks.

"I don't know. I'll have to ask Rachel. Although she's driving, so I'd have to call her, and I can't call her because then Jenna will know and –"

"Chase, sweetie, you're talking a mile a minute," Mrs. O'Donnell says sweetly and touches my back. Her eyes are the same as Jenna's, hazel and lush. Comforting. She holds up a spoonful of pink and green. "Try the watermelon salad. Let me know if it needs more lime."

I let her spoon it into my mouth. It's delicious: acidic and fresh, sweet and sour. "Perfect. It's perfect."

"You hear that, Linda? Chase thinks it's perfect."

"Oh, whatever," Mom says, taking a kitchen towel and whapping it toward Mrs. O'Donnell.

Mrs. O'Donnell squeals with laughter and goes back to her station at the kitchen island. "Your mom thought there needed to be more lime, but I told her it was perfect, so –"

"Chase, come try the sauce that's going to go on the fish and tell Kathy that it doesn't need more salt, hm?"

"I don't want to get in the middle of this," I chuckle. My phone buzzes in my pocket. I whip it out as fast as possible. A text from Rachel.

*Just finished getting Jenna a new dress at the mall. Be home in 20.*

My mouth grows hot. "They'll be here in twenty minutes," I say, almost inaudibly.

Both moms hear me, though, and immediately go into overdrive getting things in serving dishes and plating. I go back outside and announce, "Twenty minutes, guys," my voice cracking in the process.

"Oh, god, I haven't even started in on the napkins," Mr. O'Donnell moans. "I wanted to make swans!"

"Well, figure it out!" Dad calls back as he repositions a pot of flowers.

Despite the flurry of activity, I feel utterly overwhelmed. All of my excitement quickly turns to dread and I begin to think this was all a mistake. That is until Dan comes over to me. Dan's good at sensing things, sensing moods and shifts. "Hey, Chase. Take a seat. We got this."

I nod. "Okay."

"I promise," he says with a big smile. He pats me on the back and rushes over to a string of lights that has come undone and hangs limply over the fence.

I sit on a deck chair, wringing my hands together as I go over everything I want to say to her. The dread slowly melts away as I watch the finishing touches of the yard come together seamlessly. I can't help but be elated at how everyone is getting along and pitching in to make this night special. I hope that Jenna can feel all the love that's gone into this, from our mothers' recipes to our fathers' handiness. Not to mention Rachel's distraction and Dan's willingness to be the muscle for the evening. Together, they have created a dreamscape. A perfect night.

I just hope it ends perfectly as well.

16

—————

## JENNA

I stand outside the MacAllistair house with my arms crossed over my chest, idling my gaze on the front stop where just a few days ago I was in absolute bliss with Chase.

Rachel breezes past me, swinging her car key around her finger. "I just have to get changed and then we can head out." She goes up to the door and starts to unlock it.

"I'll just wait for you out here," I say, chewing on my lip.

She shoots me a look over her shoulder. "Don't be like that, Jenna."

"I could even wait in the car and pick out where we should go to dinner, I – "

"Jenna, no one else is home, I promise. Just come inside," Rachel says exasperatedly. "Don't be weird."

I can't help but smile. It would be weird of me not to go inside after all these years. Plus, the car park is empty besides the car Rachel and I came in. I wonder where Chase is if he's not home...maybe he's with his bandmates...I convince myself of that to justify why he hasn't replied yet.

I follow Rachel inside and she immediately shoots upstairs. "Be back in a minute!"

"You want me to – "

"No, stay downstairs!"

I frown. I thought maybe she'd want my opinion on her outfit so that we could make sure our vibes matched for dinner tonight. I pull down on the hem of the dress I just picked out at Abercrombie. A short green wiggle dress with a white floral pattern. It's perfect for summer, perfect for a night out to dinner. I sort of wish Chase could see me in this. He's never seen me all dressed up.

The house smells good. The MacAllistair house has a distinct smell to me after all these years; it's a comforting smell like warm milk or freshly washed sheets. But it smells differently today. Like things have been cooking in the kitchen. I peek inside. There's no one in there and the kitchen is spotless. But the dishwasher is running...

In the distance, there's music. It's coming from outside. This is all just a little...odd. Like people were here and they just evaporated into thin air.

Beyond the sliding glass doors, there's a glowing light. From the MacAllistair yard, you can often watch twilight melt over the sky, but this light is distinctly different.

I go and open the door and my jaw immediately drops.

The yard looks as I've never seen it, edged in strings of globe lights casting warmth across the yard. There are scads of flowers like I've never seen. Moon-faced sunflowers inter-mingled with a spattering of green leaves. The music is clearer now. Moaning guitar, crooning male voice. Glen Campbell, I think. One of Chase's favorites.

*It's knowing that your door is always open*
*And your path is free to walk....*

And speaking of Chase, the picture would not be

complete without him, right at the center of it all, flanking a small, well-set table. The food I smelled is more like a bounty, a feast. And he's...well, he's perfect.

"Hi, Jenna."

Chase has never looked more beautiful than he does right now. He's trimmed his beard and gotten his haircut shaped up, making him look suave and put together, yet still completely relaxed in his own way. He wears a crisp white button-down with the cuffs rolled up to his elbows, showing off his sexy forearms as well as his defined chest. And his leg is cast-free. He can stand to his full height without anything hampering him. It's...surreal.

"What...what is all this?" I ask. My heart is beating so fast that I feel like my tongue is about to swell up in my mouth.

Chase starts to approach me. I have to consciously make sure I don't back away. I don't know why I'm terrified. Maybe I'm just overwhelmed. He holds out his hand to me to help me down the stairs of the deck to the yard. "I wanted to do something for you. Is that okay?"

I bite the inside of my cheek to keep from smiling too big. I nod before I speak. "Yeah. Yes, it's – yes." I put my hand into his and feel every nerve in my body relax. I never thought I'd get to do this again.

He helps me down the stairs; my black platforms Rachel convinced me to buy now seem absolutely ridiculous for a dinner in the backyard.

"This is incredible," I say, now standing on the grass, basking in the light that makes it feel like we're surrounded by thousands of fireflies.

"It turned out really nice," he says with a proud smile. "I had a lot of help."

I suddenly feel like we're being watched. I turn to look

up at the back of the MacAllistair house and see Rachel looking at us from her bedroom window. She gasps and jerks her curtain closed. I smile to myself. I turn back to Chase and find him standing behind one of the chairs at the table.

"Would you…" he says slowly, "join me for dinner?"

My smile transforms into a grin, and I nod. "Yes, I'd love to."

Chase pulls out the chair for me and tucks it under me as I sit. I thank him, feeling his thumbs up against my shoulder blades before he pulls his hands away. For as much intimacy as we have had, the sensation of touching is new and terrifying again.

I peruse the table full of food, salivating already. There's a beautiful bone-in fish with crispy skin, skewers of roasted vegetables, roasted chickpeas, and…a watermelon salad. "Did you get the watermelon salad recipe from my mom? It looks exactly the same."

Chase shakes his head and smiles slyly. "No, your mom made it."

My eyes widen. "How did you – "

"Let me explain."

As we help ourselves with food, Chase explains how this whole night has come together. How he told his parents (and Dan) about us and how supportive they were. How after he got his cast off, the very first thing he did was walk over to my house and speak to my father about wanting to be with me. How he eventually softened Rachel's anger and made amends with her. And how each one of these people played a part in creating this night, from our dads and Dan setting up the backyard, our mothers cooking, and, of course, Rachel's distraction.

"I was wondering why Rachel was being so generous," I

giggled, watching Chase pour champagne into the flute in front of me.

"Of course, she's always generous when she's using my credit card."

I laugh and feel a wave of gratitude for Chase for giving Rachel and me that opportunity to spend so much time together in such a special way. "So, is everyone watching from the upstairs windows?"

"They are all at dinner. And Rachel should be joining them, but she might have lingered to make sure you weren't upset," he answers, filling his flute now.

"Upset? How could I be? This is all so..." I am at a loss for words. What is it? Amazing? Wonderful? Incredible? Those words all pale in comparison to the actual depth of my feeling.

Chase raises his champagne flute, suggesting a toast. I follow suit. "What should we toast to?" he asks. I can sense a bit of nervousness in his voice, like maybe he had an idea and thought better of it before saying it.

I, though, have a sudden clarity. "To tonight."

Chase's blue eyes glimmer. "To tonight."

We clink our glasses together and sip our champagne.

"Okay, the food is sufficiently cold, so dig in," Chase says wryly.

Over dinner, we talk and talk and talk. Just as we have all summer. About everything and nothing at once. We don't talk about us, at least not directly. Right now, everything feels like it's about us. Even the summer night itself feels like it's about us, and everyone in the neighborhood, in Houston, in the country, in the world, knows tonight is about Chase and me.

The food is divine. Tasty, light, fresh, and yet filling beyond compare. The watermelon salad tastes the best it ever has, but the sauce for the fish is the real star of the show. There are periods when Chase and I are utterly quiet because we are enraptured with the food. I've never had a better meal.

Once our plates are emptied and both of us stuffed (I hope my bloat doesn't show through the new dress), Chase clears the table except for the champagne, which he tops off with the dregs of the bottle. I drink it without thinking, without measuring. Even though the food is done, there's still so much on the table. It's gotten darker too; Chase grabs a small matchbook and lights two tapered candles that have been sitting on the table conspicuously. "I had so much on my mind, I forgot to light these..."

"I barely noticed," I reply.

The candles catch flame easily, flickering and flying in their gentle way. I stare at one of them. It's easier than looking at Chase; when I look at him, my pulse starts to get out of control.

"I also forgot to tell you how beautiful you look."

I feel a flush burst out across my cheeks. I look down at my dress and smooth my hands down my thighs, smiling to myself. "Thank you." Then, I raise my eyes to him and admire how even when he tries to be clean cut, his hair falls in perfect unplanned tresses, and his smile is cocky. "So do you. I mean...I forgot to tell you how...beautiful..." I trail off, our eyes locking together. We wouldn't have to say another word and I would know. I would know everything he was thinking.

"Listen, Jenna – "

"I'm sorry, I didn't text you back," I burble without thinking. "I was so mad at myself – at both of us, really, for doing that to Rachel and I just thought – "

"It's okay, Jenna. She told me she told you to stay away

from me. I understand why you didn't text," Chase says softly. For a man with such a gruff exterior who can be so intimidating in his stature, he can also be remarkably tender.

I begin to play with my napkin in my lap nervously. Chase extends his hand across the table, palm upward. His palm is wide and his fingers long. His skin looks inviting and comforting. I have held his hands many times now, but just a week apart from it fills me with exhilaration. I put my hand in his and immediately feel my entire body fill with warmth and relief. It might sound crazy, but my hand is meant to be in his. I'm meant to be with him. I don't know how I know, especially when I'm so young and don't have much experience. But I *know*.

Chase's hand wraps around mine, his thumb drifting back and forth across my skin. He smiles softly and I can tell he knows too. And that's something, considering his age and how he could truly have his pick of any woman in the world. But it's my hand in his that puts that look on his face. "Jenna," he says my name carefully as if each letter is a precious gemstone.

"Chase."

His eyes flick up to mine and his smile brightens like he's eaten something a little too sweet. "I know that things between us have been a bit unconventional from the beginning."

"You could say that," I tease.

Chase chuckles. "Well, you know, I think we both tried to keep things friendly."

"Totally. That's why you kissed me out of the blue while playing blackjack, right?"

"Listen! I tried!"

I can't help but laugh loudly.

"You always give me so much shit," Chase says, leaning his cheek into his free hand, his elbow on the table.

"I do," I affirm, then squeeze his hand. "And you love it."

Chase sighs. "I do. I really do." He admires our hands together again. "Anyway, there's clearly something more between us."

I nod. I have no words right now. I just want to see where this is going.

"And if you would be comfortable...after everything," he pauses to swallow. "I'd like to try this again. The old-fashioned way. With dates and not hiding everything and –"

"I'd like that," I answer before he finishes.

Chase lets out a breath of relief and suddenly sits up straighter. He puts his other hand over our clasped hands. "You have no idea how happy that makes me."

Even though I'm thrilled, all the what-ifs come rushing into my brain. "But your leg! I haven't even – your leg is better. So, you'll move back to your apartment."

"Well, yes – "

"And you guys are recording a new album. You'll be in the studio and – "

"I'll still be in Houston."

"And then *tour*! Oh my god, Chase, you'll go on tour and then – "

"Jenna!" Chase cuts me short with an urgency in his voice. "I want to make it work. I *will* make it work." His eyes are dancing back and forth, his hand tightening on mine. "Because I – "

Before he can finish, there's the shrill cry of a bird. Burbling, cawing. I know the sound: a hawk. I look over at the tree where the Cooper's Hawks have been keeping their nest. The female is swooping toward the yard with wide, brave wings and behind her follows one of her young, puffy, and less elegant, but still, flying.

A first flight.

I bolt up from the table and go toward the edge of the fence. "Oh my god! One of the chicks is fledging!"

One of the most precious journeys of a baby bird is the moment it decides to jump from the nest. It is an act of immense faith in oneself to be able to know that their wings are ready. That it's okay to fall because that's the only way to fly.

My heart swells as if it could get any bigger. My eyes fill with tears. The fledgling awkwardly tries its first flight, but eventually finds the grace of its mother, the perfect way to catch the air in its wings.

I feel Chase's hand on my shoulder, his body behind me. And I melt back into him, dissolve into his embrace. He rocks me back and forth, pressing a kiss to the crown of my head. "Jenna," he whispers.

"Hm?" I ask, pushing my head back against his chest.

"Jenna, I love you."

My jaw drops. I look up at him. His brow is pinched at the center, eyes crinkled at the corners with an emotion I'm not sure how to define. I don't know what to say and the silence is long enough to make him scramble.

"I know that's a lot to hear. But I can't keep it inside anymore. I love you," Chase continues, half-smiling. "You don't have to say it back, I just – "

I cut him off with a kiss. Of course, I love him. There's no question. I wrap my arms around his neck, my feet almost entirely off the ground. Chase takes me up in his arms, but his balance isn't quite back to normal yet, all that time off one leg, and we tumble to the ground, a tangle of arms and legs, curses and laughter. "You okay?" I ask, touching his leg gently.

"Yes, I'm fine, are you?"

I grin. "Better than fine." I kiss him again gently. "I love you. I love you, Chase MacAllistair."

Chase wraps his hand around my lower back, a satisfied smile on his face. He touches my chin, and runs his hand up the side of my face, his fingers tangling in my hair. "Really?"

"Really!" I say joyfully. Perhaps I sound too excited or eager, but who cares? I'm in love! I kiss him again and then laugh. "So much for going slow."

"Now, I never said *slow*..." Chase corrects. "I just said old-fashioned."

I raise an eyebrow, "So does that mean I'm saving myself for marriage?"

He closes his eyes. "I really hope not."

"Don't worry," I smirk. "I don't have that good of self-restraint."

We lay there awhile talking, giggling, cuddling on the grass as the night sinks around us. We even fall asleep right there until Rachel and Dan wake us up with flashlights. "Okay, lovebirds!" Rachel announces. "Bedtime!"

Chase walks me home; my parents greet us at the door, both treating Chase with dearness. They leave us on the porch for a final moment.

"So, you free tomorrow night?" Chase asks with a swarthy smile.

"I might be," I reply coyly, although I can't keep up an act.

"Can I take you out?"

I nod. "I'd like that."

We kiss one last time.

"Goodnight, Chase."

"Goodnight, Jenna."

Chase slowly steps away from me, walking backward, to not take his eyes off me.

"Careful," I warn. "We can't afford another broken leg."

"Wouldn't be the worst thing in the world if I get a visit from you every day, now would it be?"

I cross my arms and smile at him. "You're impossible."

He stops and looks at me. His eyes travel down my whole body. Not lasciviously, not sexually. Just taking me in entirely. From the silence, he finally speaks. "I love you."

And I echo right back, "I love you."

Absence makes the heart grow fonder. And while I've had too much absence from Chase this past week, I want tomorrow to come fast. I open the door and slip inside, looking back at him one last time with a knowing look. *Tomorrow, tomorrow, tomorrow.*

My parents don't ask. They can tell by the way I blush that things have gone well. I smile at them and trip up the stairs.

Not fifteen minutes later, my phone buzzes. Chase.

*I love you, I love you, I love you. I'll never get tired of saying it.*

§

Things move quickly from there. Chase and I begin seeing each other nearly daily again, although this time, "the old-fashioned way." I say *nearly* daily because we both have our lives to tend to. Soul Sounds prepares for the studio, I have school. Plus, we have our families and he has physical therapy sessions. Luckily, we get to spend time almost every week with both of our families together. We have loud and happy dinners full of laughter out in the MacAllistair yard. It happens so easily, feels as if we were made for this.

Rachel warms up even more to the idea of Chase and

me together. She's the one who wants to talk about it, asks (too many) questions. I have to tell her to settle down. "When are you getting married?" she teases me.

"Didn't he tell you? We already are!" I joke.

She whines, "Stoppp! I'm traumatized! Don't joke about that!"

When October starts, Chase and I do our best to balance our schedules. I'm usually done early in the day, but he and his bandmates don't get started until much later. Squeezing in time doesn't work for very long when we're both exhausted by the time we get to see each other. One night, when Chase and I are lying in bed in his lush, top-floor condo in downtown Houston, and we are tiredly trying to keep talking even though we are doomed to sleep, he suggests, "Why don't you come join me at the studio when you're done with classes?"

"Fall break isn't for another two weeks, Chase," I laugh, pushing my face into his neck, inhaling his natural, magnetic musk.

He wraps his arms around me. "No, what I mean is, why don't you come to the studio when you're done with school *every day*?"

I frown. "Well, I'll have work to do and – "

"You can do it at the studio. And when you're done, you can chill with us."

"I'd just be in the way," I reply.

"No, you wouldn't," Chase says, drawing up onto his elbow and putting a hand around my chin. He gingerly strokes the soft flat of my cheek. "Please think about it."

I kiss his thumb. "I will."

And I do. Only a couple of days later, after I've finished my botany class for the day, I make my way over to the studio. Chase meets me out front. He's dressed down more than usual, wearing a tank top and some khaki shorts. His hair is slightly sweated. "They can't wait to meet you," he says with a grin, taking me by the hand.

Even though I'm nervous beyond belief, those nerves flood away immediately once the guys see me. They welcome me with open arms, thrilled Chase has a new girlfriend, especially Jay who claims he had something to do with it since he was there the day we met. They all take good care of me, especially Lucas who tells me all about how Dylan's married to his own little sister, so he knows how complicated relationships like Chase and mine can get.

It's miraculously easy. I do my work and then make my way into the studio to watch them play. I sort of like being a groupie, a word that's significantly changed its meaning over the years. But being in the studio, getting to hear how things pan out and songs develop, watching how the guys work. It's fascinating. Not to mention sexy.

My libido, which was already intense, gets even stronger. I mean, there's a reason musicians are the most sought-after guys in the world. Watching Chase play and work is unlike anything else. The focus, the power that seeps into every one of his muscles when he's playing, it's *divine*, feels like it's bestowed upon him from God. It makes me unable to resist him. Day after day, I have to quench my appetite for him. Whether that's at his condo or in the car before we pull up to my parents' house, I have to have him.

"Do you know how many girls would be so jealous of you?" Chase asks me one day in the car after we've tangled in the backseat and we're sticky with sweat and our muscles are cramped from the ridiculous position.

"Do you think you're that special?" I shoot back with a smirk.

Chase laughs loudly, "Touché."

But I do think about that often. There are probably *plenty* of women who would be absolutely envious of my relationship with Chase.

One day, in the studio, Chase bars me from entering until they're ready. "New song," he says. "Want to get it right before anyone else hears it."

I roll my eyes. I've learned the band can be superstitious. *Artists.* Always worried that if the conditions aren't right, things will flop. I wait patiently outside until Lucas comes out to get me. Chase isn't behind the kit as usual; he's holding an acoustic guitar to compliment Dylan's electric. Lucas sits me down on the couch and joins me. "I'm sitting this one out," he says with a cheeky smile.

That's when Chase starts to play. A lilting pattern on the guitar that sounds as clear as the morning sun rising over the horizon. His blue eyes flick up to me and then away quickly. He seems so nervous, so unlike the cocky Chase I'm used to. Then, he starts to sing. I'm captivated. The words, the melody, his voice...I didn't know he could sing, let alone play guitar. But he's got a beautiful, low, almost gruff voice. It's got a quality I've never heard before. When he reaches the chorus, the meaning is abundantly clear.

*Walking tall, walking fast*
*Just know your strength, it doesn't last*
*When you break, when you fall*
*There's only one who'll be there through it all*

I can't help but laugh even though there are tears in my eyes. This is so clearly about me, for me. Lucas takes my hand as we listen. "It's good," he whispers.

And I nod in response.

Later, when Chase and I are alone, he explains to me how my presence in the studio gave him the courage to ask for a song on the album. "It's just going to be buried, you know. A deep track. But...it'll be there."

There's so much I wish I could say, but all that comes out is, "Thank you." But what I mean is, "I love you, I love you, I love you forever."

The recording finishes in November as the weather is crisping with Texas Autumn. By Christmas, the press has gotten a hold of the news: Soul Sounds' new album drops in March of next year, and Chase MacAllistair is taken. We even have a little picture in People Magazine. My mom gets it framed. I tell her it's ridiculous, but secretly, I'm happy someone did. I never thought I'd be in People Magazine.

The holidays are perfect. Our families spend Christmas eve at our house and Christmas day at Chase's. It feels like a Hallmark movie, truly special and magical. Love really does color everything a different way. Chase gets me a pair of state-of-the-art binoculars for birdwatching and I get him a personalized deck of playing cards to open with the family. That night, when we are alone, I give him his real present. A series of photos of me by a boudoir photographer. He loves it.

Along with the album, a new tour is imminent. Soul Sounds manager wants promotion and release to run simultaneously because the demand is so high, which is incredible, but terrifying. Chase and I discuss me joining him and putting classwork on hold, but that becomes impossible once I'm offered a research position in the Galapagos for the second half of the semester to study the unique bird population.

It isn't an easy conversation, but Chase is adamant I take the position. "It's what you wanted. You'll join me for the second leg in June."

After spending nearly every day with him since the

beginning of the summer, the goodbye is hard. Chase drives me to the airport and almost considers buying a ticket just to fly with me to Ecuador, but we settle for a loving goodbye before security.

"I love you. I'll call you every day."

"Every hour," I say, tears welling up in my eyes.

"Of course," he replies, his voice knotting at the back of his throat with emotion. He draws me up in his arms and kisses me, my feet off the ground. He's gotten so much stronger since his accident and his balance is back to normal.

I cry the whole flight. Once I make it to the Galapagos, I'm distracted by the incredible surroundings; I just wish I could share it with Chase. He's shown me so much of his world and I want to show him mine, out in nature.

The long-distance is tricky, especially when our schedules are so busy. But we make it work. I'm not for a second jealous or worried he's philandering while on tour. Every opportunity we get to talk is soft and loving and just...quintessentially us. We play blackjack online together and every Monday, Chase sends me flowers for my tiny box of a room at the research hostel. I send him daily pictures of the animals. I'm in heaven here. The flightless cormorants, giant tortoises, sea lions, and iguanas: it's an animal lover's paradise.

I keep up with the performances and pictures from the tour like it's my lifeblood. Every morning and every night, I troll the internet for more of my guy. Turns out, the song he wrote, which he titled, "Crutch" (a little on the nose, but it fits the vibe), is a breakout hit from the album. They play it every night in their short acoustic set, Chase taking center stage out from behind the drum kit.

Chase visits me for a short stint when he's got a break

from the tour and I take him snorkeling. For such a big guy, he's very jumpy when it comes to being in the water, scared that the fish will touch his feet.

My research assistantship goes incredibly well: I'm invited back for the Fall. I tell them I'll have to talk about it with my family once I'm back in the States. In truth, that sounds like a dream. But now I've got my other dream, the love of my life, in my other hand. Both feel so heavy with how intensely I want them. But Chase, my family...those feel just a little heavier. Those are the things I'll never want to lose.

My return to Houston lines up perfectly with Soul Sounds Houston residency. Five performances, just for their hometown. For Texas. Rachel picks me up from the airport and speeds us over to the House of Blues. Chase and I agreed I'd make it to the second performance once I'm rested from traveling, but why the hell would I wait when I can be there for this one?

I make it just in time. Rachel and I bob and weave through them to the very front where Dan has held our spots. The lights dim and Soul Sounds mills onto the stage. The welcoming sound of Chase's sticks counting them in kicks off the set and wham! The crowd is hit with a wall of sound. They are in their finest form, well-rested and ready to kick some ass.

I've been listening to them like crazy the past few months I've been gone, but that doesn't compare to how they sound live. They're electric, pulsing. Lucas fronts the band with showmanship while Dylan backs him up with finesse, complimented by the dynamic duo of the rhythm section, Jay and Chase, who bring all the power and precision they can muster.

Jay's the one who spots me in the middle of their first

song; his jaw drops and his eyes light up. After their first song, Jay's able to get Lucas's attention, and Lucas announces through the mike, "Looks like we have one of our biggest fans in the crowd, Jenna O'Donnell!"

Chase immediately shoots up off his stool, and the moment he sees me, he smiles the biggest smile possible. I wave bashfully at him, my heart full and quick.

"I'm their biggest fan," Dan says, crossing his arms disdainfully.

"Don't be jealous," Rachel replies and flicks him on the ear.

The entire performance feels like it's for me. I bask in the energy of the guys and the crowd. I'm struck with a new understanding: love is made even more potent by seeing the person you love loved by others. And when Chase comes to the front of the stage for his song and the crowd erupts, I feel like my heart is fit to burst.

Unlike the first time he sang "Crutch" for me where he could barely look at me, this time, it's *all* for me. Every lyric, every word. Once the song is over, Rachel elbows me and teases, "Ooooh, I think he likes you."

After the encore, security whisks us backstage and I get to finally see Chase. He whisks me up in his arms and spins me around. "What are you doing here?"

"Seeing you, of course!"

"But you weren't supposed to – "

"How could I miss it?" I ask, cupping his face in my hands before kissing him firmly on the lips.

This kiss, after all our time together, means something. Deep in my bones I feel it. We are about to embark on a huge adventure in just a few weeks for the second leg of his tour. A year of us knowing each other, nearly a year of being together in a sense as well. We made it. We've made it with flying colors. I'm so proud of us.

The rest of the Houston performances go off without a hitch. In fact, they're lauded by local papers as the best they've ever seen the band. "In finest form after his accident last summer," one journalist writes, "Chase MacAllistair owns the stage with his first vocal foray with Soul Sounds. This writer hopes this won't be the last we'll hear of him."

When the celebration *finally* dies down (musicians party *hard* and I learn this the hard way, with a hangover that puts me out of commission with a migraine), Chase and I are back to our old ways. We have a big dinner with both of our families to celebrate our simultaneous returns to Houston. Everyone is strangely nervous and jumpy, except for Dan who is always solid as a rock. I wonder if they're worried about Chase and me being gone all Summer. I make a note to spend extra time at home until we are scheduled to leave in June.

Life certainly changes on a dime, doesn't it? I went from despondent, single college student to a joyful, taken research assistant in under a year. And sure, I worked hard, but I think a lot of it comes down to timing and serendipity. And if there's one thing a musician knows, it's timing. Can't recommend finding one of those enough.

One evening, as I'm about to settle into dinner with my folks, there's a knock at the door. My dad goes to answer it. My mom sits up stock straight with a big smile on her face and stares at me.

"What?"

"Nothing!"

"You're smiling at me like a crazy person."

She tries to stop smiling, but she can't. "I'm not!"

"Yes, you a—" I'm cut short when I look up in the

doorway of the dining room to see Chase wearing a fantastic tan suit, hair slicked back, and a bouquet in his hand. "What are you doing here?"

"Taking you out!" my mom yelps and covers her mouth as if she wasn't supposed to say that. "Sorry, I – "

Chase laughs, "It's fine. You heard her, Jenna."

I frown and look at my dad who appears in the doorway next to Chase. "Why is everyone always in on the secret except for me?"

"Should I go? I don't have to take you out. I can give these to your mom and – " Chase says with a tone of pretend in his voice, starting to hand the flowers over to my mother.

"No!" I shout and shoot up out of my chair. "Ugh. You all are impossible."

"And you love it," Chase grins, and as I pass him, kisses the top of my head.

I giggle and shove him off. In a flurry, I get myself ready, throwing on a long, slinky black dress and tying my hair back in a way that lets a few of my curls fall around my face. "If you gave me more warning," I call out as I come down the stairs, pinning earrings into my ears as I go, "I'd be able to look nicer."

Chase shakes his head and beams. "You look perfect."

Mom and Dad stand in the hall with him, wearing the same stupid smiles. I shake it off; I'm just glad they're still infatuated with our relationship. Their approval means everything. "Have fun! Be safe!" my mom says, kissing us both on the cheeks before seeing us out the front door.

Chase leads me over to his car. He's changed his other one to the latest model of a high-end sports car. And I have to say, while I've never understood the desire for fancy cars, riding this one is a whole other ballgame. "Where are we going?" I ask.

Chase wraps his wide hand around the gearshift and smiles mischievously, "It's a surprise."

"And somehow, I'm *not* surprised," I say under my breath.

We drive only a short bit; Chase turns his car into the parking lot of the Greenpoint strip mall and parks in front of the Mexican joint with the striped awning. I remember the first time I brought him tacos from there; ever since, we get it almost weekly.

I start laughing. "We got dressed up for dinner in a strip mall?"

"No," Chase says defensively. "We got dressed up to pick up dinner at the strip mall. There's a difference. Just one minute."

Chase gets out of the car and is back in a flash, carrying a huge brown bag that's full to the brim with tacos, queso, chips, and elote. I can smell it once he puts it in the backseat and it smells divine. I could honestly start eating them now if I wasn't worried about getting salsa on the leather seats.

"And, of course –" He puts two cups of horchata in the cup holders. The largest size they have.

I smile over at him skeptically. Something is going on here. "Where are we going, Chase?"

"You'll see," he says, eyes twinkling.

I try not to ask any more questions. Chase drives us downtown and we park near Discovery Green, the public park that's a sort of jewel of downtown Houston. He pulls a picnic blanket out of the trunk as well as a bottle of rum to make the horchata "fun" as he says. We walk through the park, me in high heels trying not to get stuck in the dirt.

We set up camp near one of the small waterways. It's simultaneously metropolitan and idyllic here in the park. To be able to sit near the water and hear it rippling and look up at the sky and see towering buildings is strange but comforting. Houston. Home. It's a good home. I'm excited to travel with Chase on tour, but Houston will always be home.

"What's the special occasion?" I ask as I distribute foil-wrapped tacos between us.

Chase's eyebrows jump. "Can't I just do something nice for you?"

"Well, you always do nice things for me," I say with a chuckle and a sip of horchata.

"So, then what makes this any different?"

I look out over the park. It's a beautiful early spring night. Older folks taking walks, couples on benches, families laughing and playing games of catch. I guess there isn't anything different about a nice night out with Chase. But for some reason, tonight feels different. Something in the air. Something about how Chase is keeping everything to himself.

Maybe...no. I push the thought of a proposal from my mind. It's too fast, too soon. I'd say yes of course, but it's just not happening tonight.

After I push the thought away, we enjoy dinner and each other's company as we always do. Halfway through, an older woman on the arm of her husband calls out to us from across the green, "You two are beautiful together!"

I blush and smile at Chase and he calls back, "Thank you, although it's all her, I promise!"

"Chase..." I say bashfully.

"Thatta boy," the husband says with a grin.

They give us a wave as they continue their evening walk.

"You're a flatterer," I say to him.

Chase shakes his head. "Not lying."

"You're the one who's – "

"That doesn't mean anything. You take the sticks out of my hand. Make me an accountant or a lawyer. I'm not as handsome as you think, trust me," Chase says with a shrug.

I crinkle my nose at him and then lunge for him, wrapping my arms around his neck and pushing him down on the blanket. He yelps into laughter. "You're so full of shit!" I squeal and then pepper kisses all over his face as I say, "You know you'd be the sexiest accountant-lawyer-barista-whatever."

Chase turns red, even under his beard. He puts his hand on the small of my back and pulls me close to him. "It's good to know that you'd still love me even if I was a normal guy."

I put my hand on his chest and look up at the sky. It's dark now, but the city lights create a bright dome around us. Sure, we can't see the stars, but it's a different sort of romance. Chase *is* a normal guy to me. His work as a drummer hasn't ever been the thing that pulled me to him. It was just who he was from the very moment he stepped out of Jay's car a year ago. "I'd love you no matter what, Chase."

He sighs blithely and runs his hand up and down my back. "You're such a special person, Jenna. And...I'm so grateful you're coming on tour with me. It means everything to me."

I nuzzle my face into his chest. "I wouldn't miss it for the world." There's a pang in my heart. I still haven't told him about the Fall, about potentially going back to the Galapagos. I had honestly convinced myself I wouldn't say anything about it and refuse the research position. But the dishonesty doesn't sit right with me. "So...I have something to tell you."

"Me too," he says with an urgency in his voice that doesn't match how we are languishing on the picnic blanket.

I sit up slightly so I can look into his eyes. "You go first."

"No, no, you," Chase says.

I swallow. "So, my research assistantship. It went really well. So well that they've invited me back for next semester."

Chase smiles, but his brow flinches the slightest bit. I know that bittersweet feeling of being pulled in two directions. "Jenna, that's fantastic."

"But I think I'm going to turn it down."

His frown wins out over his smile. "What? Why?"

"Because, well, it's so complicated, you know? It was hard being away from you."

The wrinkles in Chase's forehead soften. "Jenna..."

"And at least if I'm in Houston doing classwork, then even if you have to leave, you'll always come home to me. Versus me being in South America, I mean – "

"Jenna, we don't know what's going to happen," Chase says. It's comforting and discomforting at the same time. But he says it with such ease that I feel safe. "With the album going well, who knows what the tour is going to look like after the summer. *If* we'll tour after the summer. I mean, I could always come down to stay with you if I have the time."

I scoff, "Chase, the album is huge. You know that won't be possible."

"It might be," he says, sitting up. "We don't know."

I chew on my lower lip. It's one thing if we have to work

with his unfathomable schedule. But mine too? It seems too much.

Chase grabs my hands in his. "I'm committed to making this work. Regardless of where life takes us. Literally... metaphorically..."

I giggle, feeling my eyes fill with tears.

"Do you want to do it?" he asks softly.

*Yes.* I don't feel like I can say it aloud. It's the first time I've actually known the answer. Yes, there is a part of my heart there. I still have so much I want to do there. I'm just so scared that means sacrificing so much or that things will fracture, and we won't be able to fix it like a broken leg. But he asked, and I won't lie to him. "Yes," I reply.

A tear escapes one of my eyes and before I can catch it, he brushes it away with his thumb. "Then you'll do it."

I look into his eyes. Big, icy blue that used to feel so cold and unattainable. Now, they're my home. My life. I hope forever. "You sure?"

"Of course," Chase replies. I know there's no question in his mind by the sound of his voice. "I love you, Jenna. For every part of you. I would never ever ask you to close up a part of yourself because you're scared of losing me. Because I'm not going anywhere, ever. I promise."

I smile, even though tears are streaming down my face. How did I get so lucky?"

"And —" his voice falters, and he looks away suddenly. "Give me a second."

Chase withdraws from me, turning away. I don't know what to do with my hands. I can't tell if something's wrong, or —

"I was going to wait until a bit later, but..." Chase reaches into his jacket and turns back around, shifting onto bended knee. In his hands, he holds a small burgundy ring box, and suddenly, I know what's happening.

I back away reflexively, my heart pounding, my head spinning.

"Okay, here it goes," he says with a nervous smile.

I rise onto my knees, thinking I should stand, but my legs are like Jell-O.

"Jenna. Meeting you made me realize that life is nothing without love. And regardless of what the rest of my life looks like, I know it will be beautiful every day with you in it."

If I wasn't crying before, I'm certainly crying now. I have to cover my mouth to not sound like I'm choking on my saliva.

"You're compassionate and hilarious and can be a pain in my ass – "

I laugh loudly, clutching my hands to my heart thinking of all the moments I've given him shit.

"And I can't imagine my life without you. So..." Chase pops open the box; I'm practically blinded by the diamonds encrusted in the ring. He takes a deep breath and licks his lips. "Will you marry me?"

I don't know if I actually say yes before I throw my arms around him and kiss him. Inside, every nerve in my body has answered for me. There's no hesitation...it's implicit.

Yes, yes, yes.

## 17

## CHASE

THE RING FITS PERFECTLY. SLIDING IT ONTO JENNA'S finger is like a dream come true. I've had the ring for...well... an embarrassingly long time. Since Christmas. I had thought about proposing to her then, but Rachel told me not to. Her actual words were, "You've been in a relationship since August, slow down."

And I'm glad I waited, even if we didn't make it to a year before I asked. In that time, Jenna and I both have grown so much and discovered so much about ourselves and each other. "We can wait until you're done with school to plan the wedding," I say, even though in my heart of hearts I want her to be my wife as soon as possible.

Jenna twiddles her fingers, watching how the light glints off the diamonds on the ring. "I knew you were acting funny. You *all* were acting funny."

I chuckle. "Guilty as charged."

She looks at me with her lips twisted. "I hate you."

"I love you too," I reply and kiss her on the side of the head.

From across the park, the old couple that had passed us

early lets out excited yells and claps their hands. Jenna and I shyly thank them. I take Jenna's hand in my hand and feel my heart flutter at the coolness of the ring on her finger. I pull her hand up to my lips and kiss it gently. "Come on. I have one more surprise."

"More?" she says, her voice gliding upward. "I don't know how much more I can take!"

"I'm resisting every urge to make a dirty joke but – "

"Oh my *god*, you're so bad."

"And you love it."

She smiles begrudgingly. "What's the surprise?"

We go back to the car, and as soon as she gets in the passenger seat, my heart starts thudding. Note to self: one major life surprise per evening in the future.

I know the route by heart by this point and don't need a map, but I end up driving in circles, trapped in the downtown one-ways, until Jenna finally gets me to the highway. "Sorry," I say, sheepishly. "I'm nervous."

"What for?" Jenna asks, her hazel eyes seeming greener in the city light. "You've already got me."

That settles my pulse just the slightest bit. Yes. I do. From the corner of my eye, as I drive, I see Jenna admire the ring on her hand. Getting used to it as if it's a tattoo or a piercing, except it's bigger than that. It's a whole new limb, an extension of me. Of us.

Neither of us has much to say. We're both simply emanating joy. But after a while of driving in silence, Jenna pops the radio on. As if by magic, "Crutch" starts to play on the radio from the middle of the chorus. She looks over at me, her eyes wide, like a child watching a bunny appear out of a hat.

"I had nothing to do with it, I promise," I say wryly.

"Sure, you didn't," she says and puts her hand on the

back of my neck. She brushes her fingernails through my hair and begins to hum along. It's her song. I've never told her as much since it's abundantly clear from the lyrics, from the way I presented it to her all those months ago. I might have called the song "Jenna" if our manager didn't nix the title for being too sappy.

"Crutch" takes us out of the intense cityscape to the more residential portion of town, a few neighborhoods over from our families. It's not as bougie as River Oaks or any of the elite neighborhoods. This one's more friendly.

"Where are you taking me?" Jenna asks, suspicion creeping into her voice.

In my head, I answer, *home.*

After Jenna left for Ecuador and just before I went on the first leg of the tour, I was intent on finding us a place where we could root ourselves. That no matter where we went, we could always come home. To our home. Not my condo downtown. Not our parents' homes. Somewhere quintessentially for us. And after narrowing it down to just a few options, I took the whole MacAllistair-O'Donnell clan to see the options.

They settled on a beautiful, light blue bungalow ready for a huge remodel. Bigger than a standard bungalow, with a sprawling backyard that's surrounded by trees. The thing that sold them was the veranda when Rachel burst into tears inexplicably. When she calmed down, she smiled with wistfulness in her eyes: "I can see you two growing old here. In rocking chairs on the porch."

And while there's a lot between now and us getting old, I have to admit, I saw it.

I pull the car in front of the house, which looks exactly as I remember it, except the sign in the yard has changed from "For Sale" to "Sold."

"We're here," I say softly.

Jenna looks at the house and then back at me, frowning. "Here where?"

I smile. "Come on."

We get out of the car, and I lead her up the front walkway, past the mailbox with the house number and cleanly kept yews. I make my way up to the front door and am about to reach into my pocket for the key, but Jenna suddenly squeaks, "Chase! What are you doing?"

I turn around. She hasn't climbed the steps yet, her arms nervously crossed over her chest, looking around at the neighboring houses. "Why are you whispering?"

"Because it's late and we look like creeps or robbers or something," Jenna answers, her head bobbing with emphasis on every word.

I laugh loudly and reach into my pocket, withdrawing the key to the front door that dangles on a silly duck key chain given to me by the realtor. "Are you ready for the second surprise?"

Jenna's face changes from incredulity to complete and utter shock. "You didn't."

I unlock and open the door in a fluid motion before smiling smugly at her. "I'm afraid I did."

Jenna's frozen to her spot, unable to comprehend what's just happened.

"Come on inside," I say, gesturing to the open doorway.

She doesn't move. She looks up at the façade of the house, over at the cobblestone driveway, and shakes her head as if she can't believe her eyes.

"Alright, if you insist..." I say with a roll of my eyes. I go down to meet her and sweep her up in my arms, bridal style. "It might be a little unconventional to do this before the wedding, but – "

"Chase, put me down!" she says through a loud cackle, kicking her legs gently.

She feels as light as a feather in my arms. It must be the adrenaline coursing through my veins from the rollercoaster of this night. I carry her up the steps to the front door. Before I step through, I look at her: "You ready?"

Jenna investigates the house. There's excitement on her face, the kind she gets when she spots a bird with her binoculars. "I think so."

I step over the threshold and into the house. Our home. I give her a small kiss and then gently put her down. Jenna wanders a few steps inside. "I know it's not much," I say timidly; I forgot most of the interior is a mess with skeletons of walls and unfinished floorboards. "At least not yet."

Jenna goes into the living room and follows it to the dining room which loops into the kitchen and back into the front hall.

"But I wanted to find a place that we could finish together. You know. Really make it ours."

She smiles. "I love that idea."

"Right. We can add walls or build onto the back. The basement would be a great place for a recording studio and there's an attic we could insulate for your office or –" I'm getting ahead of myself, but I'm too excited. I've thought through it all so many times. "It's only about twenty minutes away from our folks too. So, it's private, but close."

Jenna goes over to the staircase that leads up to the second floor. She touches the newel post, looking up. Without another word, she starts to climb the stairs. I follow her, frenetically turning on the lights as she goes.

"There's three bedrooms up here and one on the first floor. Guest rooms or for..." I stop before I say children. It's something we've discussed, but with how young Jenna is, it won't happen for several years. I don't want to scare her off. "There's no rush, of course. It should be perfect. You know. Ours."

She peers into the rooms that flank the stairs, which I've already imagined for our children.

"And this —" I go past her to the door at the end of the short hall. "Is the master." I prop open the door for her.

Jenna smiles at me before she goes inside and immediately her jaw drops. It's a huge room with vaulted ceilings and big-picture windows.

"I know it's hard to picture with no furniture, but I mean..." I explain, spreading my arms to indicate all the space.

"It's perfect," Jenna speaks abruptly. "But you didn't have to do this."

I smile at her and close the space between us, pushing the dark curls of her hair out of her face and cupping her cheeks in my hands. "I wanted to give us a place that we always have to come back to, Jens. No matter where we go or what we're doing, this is where we know we belong."

"The nest," she says with a glimmering smile.

"The nest...yeah..." I grin. "I like that." And I kiss her softly. I must have kissed her a million times and it only gets better.

Jenna breaks away and moves further into the room. The wooden floors creak under her feet. "Where would the bed go?"

I shrug. "I don't know. Probably up against that wall? Away from the door."

Jenna looks to where I've pointed. She slowly walks to the spot. "Right here?"

"Yeah. Maybe."

She looks over her shoulder at me with a devilish grin

before sinking down to the floor and laying on her back. She lifts her hands over her head and stretches her body out, showing off her beautiful curves. "Right here?" she repeats.

I don't know what to say. I only know I could lose myself in her right now on the floor of our home.

"Pretend you've just come home. And I'm sleeping and you're trying not to wake me up when you come in the room."

I laugh. She keeps me young, that's for sure. "Okay." I go out of the room and come back in, tiptoeing across the floor. I start to remove my jacket.

"Chase?" Jenna asks, her voice laden with the fake sound of exhaustion.

I laugh again.

"Shhh! Take it seriously!"

"I am, I am, I...didn't mean to wake you up."

Jenna extends one of her arms out to me. And even though she's laying on the floor, I can picture her in bed amidst a cushy bounty of pillows. "Come to bed, baby."

I drop my coat and get to my knees beside her. I wrap her up in my arms, spooning her from behind. We both look out the picture windows to the dark night. Our view in our home. "I love you," I whisper in her ear.

Jenna runs a hand up my forearm. "I love you."

I lean on my elbow, looking down at her. Jenna's eyes squint at me as if she's drunk with happiness. I brush my knuckles against her cheek and, in response, she traps my hand against her face. She kisses each one of my knuckles. "Make love to me, Chase."

My lips part. "Right here?"

Jenna nods and guides my hand from her face to her groin. I feel the heat even before I touch her. "Love me," she repeats.

There are so many ways to love Jenna. And this is just one. I have to say it's one of my favorites, but it's just one. There, on the floor of what will be our bedroom in what will be our home, we make love, just as she asked. It's slow and ponderous. She takes me deep inside her and we hold each other as close as possible, trading kisses and breaths as if we share the same lungs. Once we are both unwinding, ready to release, the only words we can find are "I love you" over and over again until the growing heat hits us both.

I want her forever. In every way, shape, and form. And I want to be hers.

While we lay there in the afterglow, I engulf her hand in mine, looking at the engagement ring on her finger. I run my thumb along the facets and the stones.

Jenna hooks her hands around my shoulders and presses her face into my neck. "Welcome home," she whispers.

And what she doesn't know is that *my* home will never be this house. It won't be the walls, the ceilings, the floorboards, the furniture.

No, my home will always be Jenna.

# EPILOGUE
## JENNA

*5 Years Later*

The morning light seeps in through the Venetian blinds, rousing me to wake. I blink my eyes open and feel Chase spooning me from behind, warm and tender. His breath is still heavy with sleep.

I gently stroke his hand that rests against my hip. "Good morning..." I coo softly.

"Mmgh," he grunts. "I'm still sleeping."

"But it's your birthday," I say, turning my face toward him, the scruff of his beard rubbing up against my chin.

Chase sighs and buries his head in the pillow. "Don't remind me..."

I giggle. Chase has been dreading this day all year. His fortieth birthday. He doesn't look it, that's for sure, except for the few silver hairs he finds and holds out to me like he's dying. "Big day ahead of you, Chasey," I say and then kiss him on the nose before leaping out of bed and pulling the blinds up.

"Oh, fuck," he snaps as the light floods the room eagerly and then he groans. "Can't I sleep in on my birthday?"

I look back at him, across the bedroom: it came together perfectly. A haven of white and cream where we can find our respite after long days or being apart. Since we were married after my graduation, Soul Sounds has come out with another two albums and done a yearlong world tour which I accompanied him on for quite some time before I was offered a research position at the Houston Audubon. Luckily, Chase was right about the house. The bungalow, which we had tailor-made to all our needs, serves as our perfect home base. Like a lighthouse calling us back to Houston again and again.

"Nope," I say with a jolly grin. "You have a full day planned. Brunch at your parents' house with our families, huge party tonight...not to mention time with little old me."

Chase's face morphs from a glower into a smile. He extends his arms across the bed into the spot I had once occupied. "Can you lay with me a little longer? As a birthday present?"

I smile askew and roll my eyes. "Ten minutes."

"Fifteen."

"Eight."

"Jenna, that's not fair."

"We're negotiating!" I laugh. "Of course, it's fair."

Chase harrumphs into the pillow. "Fine. Eight."

I go back over to the bed and sit on the edge with my legs dangling over the side. I run my hand through his blonde locks and then kiss his temple. "I'll give you ten since it's a special day."

"Thank you," he pouts, wrapping his arms around my waist and pressing his face into my lap.

I was going to wait until later in the day to tell him the news so we didn't have to sit on the excitement through brunch with our families. Rachel is going to be able to sense

I have a secret without me so much as breathing. But it doesn't feel right to keep it from him longer than I already have. "You're going to have to get better about getting up once the baby arrives."

Chase chuckles, not catching my meaning. "What's that supposed to mean?"

I don't respond and wait for him to work it out.

He sits up suddenly and looks at me with wide eyes. "Jenna, what's that supposed to mean?" he repeats, except this time he knows and just needs me to say it.

I smile at him, my eyes filling with tears before I'm even able to speak. "I'm pregnant."

Chase's eyes crinkle at the sides, and his lips part into a disbelieving smile. "Don't lie to me, Jenna."

"I'm not," I say.

"Don't joke," he replies, his voice cracking and tears flooding into his eyes.

"Chase, I promise. Look." I reach into my bedside table and pull out the positive test. "I just took it yesterday. I took four of them, I promise."

Chase takes it from me and stares at it. He puts a hand to his mouth. "Oh my god." His blue eyes dance across the test, shimmering with tears. "I can't believe it."

We haven't been trying long. After all, it's been a busy five years with my budding career and his travels. And he's always been so patient, wanting me to pursue my dreams first and foremost. But now that we're established here and things are slowing down for the foreseeable future, it made sense to finally get our family started.

"Happy birthday," I say in a small voice.

The dam bursts and tears start rolling down his face, catching in his beard. But he wears the biggest smile I've ever seen. "Come here," he says, sweetly engulfing me in his arms and pressing a kiss to my lips. He runs his hands back over my head, threading his fingers through my hair, cradling me as if I'm fragile and delicate. "You're serious?"

I brush tears out from under his eyes. "I wouldn't joke about this, Chase. Would never."

Chase puts his hands on my waist and then lifts the fabric of my tank top to reveal my belly. He touches it gingerly; even though nothing's obviously changed yet, his touch is so entirely different, feels so different. Protective and tender. "You're going to have my baby?" he asks.

I nod, beaming at him.

His skepticism suddenly evaporates and a big grin spreads out across his face. "I think my fortieth birthday might be my best yet."

I laugh and throw my arms around him. We lay in bed much longer than the ten minutes I had promised him, basking in the glow of our future together. His hand rests on my stomach and he kisses me gently from time to time. The sun begins to lap at the edge of the bed, letting us know it's beyond time to get up. But before we do, Chase whispers, "I don't know how it's possible, but I love you more every day."

I tighten his hand to my stomach. There will be hard times ahead, most certainly. But if we can commit to loving each other just a bit harder every day for the rest of our lives...I don't see how we can fail.